MW01489542

Selected Canterbury Tales

The General Prologue
The Pardoner's Introduction, Prologue and Tale
The Wife of Bath's Prologue and Tale

Geoffrey Chaucer

Edited and translated into modern English by

Simon D Pratt

Thrifty Classic Literature

Selected Canterbury Tales for Students

By Geoffrey Chaucer

Edited and translated by Simon D Pratt

Thrifty Classic Literature is a copyrighted trademark and trading style of McGowan Publications, 2018.

This edition first published in 2018 © McGowan Publications, 2018

McGowan Publications
244 Madison Avenue 10016-2817 New York City NY, USA

Email: enquiries@mcgowanpublications.com
www.mcgowanpublications.com

Translated text © Simon D Pratt, 2018

The moral right of the translator has been asserted

DEDICATION

This book is dedicated to my long-suffering
wife and daughter, Fiona and Tamsin -
also also to my dear brother Clive.

Felix culpa.

Table of Contents

Translator's Preface

Written between 1387 and 1400, Chaucer's Canterbury Tales is set on a journey made by thirty-one pilgrims (including Chaucer and the host, Harry Bailey) as they travel from Southwark in London to Thomas Becket's shrine at Canterbury. There, in return for the prize of a free dinner, the pilgrims each agreed to participate in a story-telling contest to help make their long journey more enjoyable.

This volume contains three of Chaucer's most popular tales; the General Prologue, the Pardoner's Tale and the Wife of Bath's Tale. All of these are complete and unabridged with numbered lines.

The modern translation contained in this book is based upon a literal, word-for-word approach. Here, readers will find each translated line is placed directly opposite to its Middle English counterpart. This means the meaning of unfamiliar words can be checked immediately - thereby making the present version particularly useful for those who are new to Middle English. Unfortunately, there are instances when this word-for-word approach might not provide the reader with a clear understanding of Chaucer's meaning. In these situations, an explanatory word or phrase has been added to the original text. However, these additions are clearly separated from the original text by being contained in square brackets [ ]. Furthermore, mention must also be made of one further departure from Chaucer's text. In the interests of propriety, any offensive references to female genitalia have been translated into much more acceptable language.

Many modern translations of the Canterbury Tales retain Chaucer's iambic pentameter and rhyming couplet structure. In many ways, that is a highly laudable endeavour. Unfortunately, there are instances where Chaucer's poetic framework has been preserved by transferring content from neighbouring lines,, or by inserting either a new or a substitute word which affects its presumed meaning. The word-for-word translation contained in the present book expressly avoids those difficulties; but does so at the risk of raising a criticism that it lacks a consistent structure. Clearly, some lines rhyme, whilst others do not. That said, there is one reason why the creation of a non-rhyming version of the Canterbury Tales might not be quite so seditious as first appears. The reader is reminded that Chaucer wrote his Canterbury Tales before the Great Vowel Shift of 1400 to 1600. As a result, that evolution in English pronunciation suggests the Canterbury Tales had already begun to lose it original poetic resonance soon after being written.

Whilst the greatest debt is owed to the labours of Geoffrey Chaucer himself, gratitude is also due to the scholars who contributed to the University of Michigan's electronic Middle English Dictionary. The digital MED is an outstanding achievement, and to whom this work is respectfully co-dedicated.

Simon D Pratt

Beziers, February 2018

The translator was educated at St Chad's College Durham, Warwick, Exeter and De Montfort Universities. Lately, he was both a Hardwicke and Sir Thomas More scholar of Lincoln's Inn, London. His publications include works on English law and literature.

The General Prologue

Here bygynneth the Book of the Tales of Caunterbury

Whan that Aprill, with his shoures soote

The droghte of March hath perced to the roote

And bathed every veyne in swich licour,

Of which vertu engendred is the flour;

5   Whan Zephirus eek with his sweete breeth

Inspired hath in every holt and heeth

The tendre croppes, and the yonge sonne

Hath in the Ram his halfe cours yronne,

And smale foweles maken melodye,

10   That slepen al the nyght with open eye-

(So priketh hem Nature in hir corages);

Thanne longen folk to goon on pilgrimages

And palmeres for to seken straunge strondes

To ferne halwes, kowthe in sondry londes;

15   And specially from every shires ende

Of Engelond, to Caunterbury they wende,

The hooly blisful martir for to seke

That hem hath holpen, whan that they were seeke.

Bifil that in that seson, on a day,

20   In Southwerk at the Tabard as I lay

Redy to wenden on my pilgrymage

To Caunterbury with ful devout corage,

At nyght was come into that hostelrye

Wel nyne and twenty in a compaignye

25   Of sondry folk, by aventure yfalle

In felaweshipe, and pilgrimes were they alle,

That toward Caunterbury wolden ryde.

The chambres and the stables weren wyde,

And wel we weren esed atte beste;

Here begins the Book of the Tales of Canterbury

> When April comes with his sweet showers
>
> And pierces the drought of March to the root
>
> And bathed each vein in such liquid,
>
> By whose power the flower is so produced;
>
> 5   Also, when the West Wind's sweet breath
>
> Has blown into every grove and heath
>
> The tender shoots, and the young sun
>
> Has run half of its course into Aries,
>
> And small birds make music,
>
> 10   That sleep through the night with open eyes-
>
> (So as Nature urges them with their desires);
>
> Then folk long to go on pilgrimage
>
> And professional pilgrims go in search of foreign shores
>
> To distant shrines well known in sundry lands;
>
> 15   And specially from every county's end
>
> Of England, to Canterbury they went,
>
> To seek the holy blessed martyr
>
> Who has helped them when they were sick .

> One day that season, it happened that,
>
> 20   I rested in Southwark, at the Tabard Inn
>
> Ready to start upon my pilgrimage
>
> To Canterbury, full of devout spirit,
>
> At nightfall, there came to that hostelry
>
> Some twenty nine in a company
>
> 25   Of sundry persons who had chanced to fall
>
> Into fellowship, and they were all pilgrims,
>
> Who would ride towards Canterbury.
>
> The rooms and stables were spacious and wide,
>
> And we were accommodated to the best;

30	And shortly, whan the sonne was to reste,
	So hadde I spoken with hem everichon
	That I was of hir felaweshipe anon,
	And made forward erly for to ryse
	To take our wey, ther as I yow devyse.
35	But nathelees, whil I have tyme and space,
	Er that I ferther in this tale pace,
	Me thynketh it acordaunt to resoun
	To telle yow al the condicioun
	Of ech of hem, so as it semed me,
40	And whiche they weren, and of what degree,
	And eek in what array that they were inne;
	And at a knyght than wol I first bigynne.

	A KNYGHT ther was, and that a worthy man,
	That fro the tyme that he first bigan
45	To riden out, he loved chivalrie,
	Trouthe and honour, fredom and curteisie.
	Ful worthy was he in his lordes werre,
	And therto hadde he riden, no man ferre,
	As wel in cristendom as in hethenesse,
50	And evere honoured for his worthynesse.
	At Alisaundre he was, whan it was wonne.
	Ful ofte tyme he hadde the bord bigonne
	Aboven alle nacions in Pruce;
	In Lettow hadde he reysed, and in Ruce,
55	No Cristen man so ofte of his degree.
	In Gernade at the seege eek hadde he be
	Of Algezir, and riden in Belmarye.
	At Lyeys was he and at Satalye,
	Whan they were wonne; and in the Grete See
60	At many a noble armee hadde he be.

30   *And briefly, when the sun had set,*

          I had spoken with every one of them

          Such that I immediately joined their fellowship,

          And made agreement that we would rise early

          To take our journey, about which I will contrive to tell you.

35   *But none the less, while I have the time and space,*

          [And] before I take any further step in this tale,

          I think it accords with sound reason

          To inform you about the situation

          Of each of them, as it appeared to me,

40   *Who they were, and what was their social rank,*

          And also how they were dressed;

          And I will first begin with a knight.

          A KNIGHT there was, and he a worthy man,

          That from the time when he first began

45   *To ride out, he loved chivalry,*

          Truth, honour, nobility and graciousness.

          He was highly distinguished in his lord's war,

          And thereto no man had ridden further,

          As well in Christendom as in heathen's lands,

50   *And was honoured everywhere for his distinctions.*

          He was at Alexandria, when it was captured.

          And very often sat at the head of the table

          In Prussia above the knights of all nations;

          He had fought In Lithuania and Russia,

55   *[Which] no Christian man of his rank had done so regularly.*

          He was also at the siege of Grenada

          Of Algeciras, and had ridden in Almeria.

          At Ayas was he and at Antalia,

          When they were won; and in the Mediterranean

60   *He had been on many military expeditions.*

At mortal batailles hadde he been fiftene,

And foughten for oure feith at Tramyssene

In lystes thries, and ay slayn his foo.

This ilke worthy knyght hadde been also

65   Somtyme with the lord of Palatye

Agayn another hethen in Turkye.

And everemoore he hadde a sovereyn prys;

And though that he were worthy, he was wys,

And of his port as meeke as is a mayde.

70   He nevere yet no vileynye ne sayde

In al his lyf unto no maner wight.

He was a verray, parfit gentil knyght.

But, for to tellen yow of his array,

His hors were goode, but he was nat gay.

75   Of fustian he wered a gypon

Al bismotered with his habergeoun,

For he was late ycome from his viage,

And wente for to doon his pilgrymage.

With hym ther was his sone, a yong SQUIER,

80   A lovyere and a lusty bacheler;

With lokkes crulle, as they were leyd in presse.

Of twenty yeer of age he was, I gesse.

Of his stature he was of evene lengthe,

And wonderly delyvere, and of greet strengthe.

85   And he hadde been somtyme in chyvachie

In Flaundres, in Artoys, and Pycardie,

And born hym weel, as of so litel space,

In hope to stonden in his lady grace.

Embrouded was he, as it were a meede,

90   Al ful of fresshe floures, whyte and reede;

Syngynge he was, or floytynge, al the day,

5

He had fought in fifteen mortal battles,

And he had jousted for our faith at Tlemcen

Three times in lists, and each time he'd slain his foe.

This self-same worthy knight had also been

65 At one time, fighting with the emir of Palatye

Against another heathen in Turkey.

And he always had an excellent reputation;

Though he was brave, he was also wise,

And bore himself as meekly as a maid.

70 He never spoke a rude word

In all his life, to whatsoever person.

He was a truly perfect, gracious knight.

But now, to tell you about his clothing,

His horses were good, but he did not dress gaily.

75 He wore a tunic made of coarse cloth

Stained with rust by his chain-mail jacket,

For he had recently returned from his campaign,

And was now going on his pilgrimage.

With him there was his son, a youthful SQUIRE,

80 A lover and an attractive bachelor;

With well-curled hair, as if they'd been laid in press.

I guess he was twenty years of age.

In stature he was of an average height,

Wondrously agile, and of great strength.

85 He had sometimes ridden with the cavalry

In Flanders, in Artois, and Picardy,

And had borne himself well, within that short space of time,

In hope of winning his lady's favour.

He was embroidered, as if he were a meadow,

90 Full of fresh flowers, all white and red;

He sang or played the flute all day long,

He was as fressh as is the monthe of May.

Short was his gowne, with sleves longe and wyde.

Wel koude he sitte on hors, and faire ryde.

95 He koude songes make, and wel endite,

Juste, and eek daunce, and weel purtreye and write.

So hoote he lovede, that by nyghtertale

He slepte namoore than dooth a nyghtyngale.

Curteis he was, lowely, and servysable,

100 And carf biforn his fader at the table.

A YEMAN hadde he and servantz namo

At that tyme, for hym liste ride soo;

And he was clad in cote and hood of grene.

A sheef of pecok arwes, bright and kene

105 Under his belt he bar ful thriftily,

(Wel koude he dresse his takel yemanly:

Hise arwes drouped noght with fetheres lowe)

And in his hand he baar a myghty bowe.

A not heed hadde he, with a broun visage,

110 Of woodecraft wel koude he al the usage.

Upon his arm he baar a gay bracer,

And by his syde a swerd and a bokeler,

And on that oother syde a gay daggere

Harneised wel and sharpe as point of spere.

115 A Cristopher on his brest of silver sheene.

An horn he bar, the bawdryk was of grene;

A forster was he, soothly, as I gesse.

Ther was also a Nonne, a PRIORESSE,

That of hir smylyng was ful symple and coy;

120 Hir gretteste ooth was but by Seinte Loy;

And she was cleped Madame Eglentyne.

He was as fresh as is the month of May.

His gown was short with long and wide sleeves.

He could be sit on a horse well, and rode handsomely.

95   *He could make songs and composed well,*

Joust, and dance too, as well as sketch and write.

He was so passionate as a lover, that by night

He slept no more than a nightingale.

He was courteous, humble, and helpful,

100   *And carved before his father at the table.*

He had a YEOMAN, but no more servants

At that time, for that is how he so chose to travel;

And he was clad in a green coloured coat and hood.

A sheaf of peacock arrows bright and keen

105   *[Which] he carried very suitably under his belt,*

(He could look after his equipment in a yeomanly way:

His arrows didn't fall short due to drooping feathers)

And in his hand he held a powerful bow.

He had a cropped head and a sun-browned face,

110   *In woodcraft, he knew all the proper skills.*

Upon his arm he wore an elegant wrist guard,

And by his side, a sword and a small shield,

And on the other side, an elegant dagger

Beautifully ornamented and sharp as the point of a spear.

115   *On his chest he wore a St Christopher medal of shiny silver.*

He carried a hunting horn with a green shoulder strap;

I guess that he was truly a forester.

There was also a Nun, a PRIORESS,

Who, in her smiling, was modest and coy;

120   *Her greatest oath was but by Saint Eloy;*

And she was called as Madam Eglantine.

Ful weel she soong the service dyvyne,

Entuned in hir nose ful semely,

And Frenssh she spak ful faire and fetisly,

125   After the scole of Stratford-atte-Bowe,

For Frenssh of Parys was to hir unknowe.

At mete wel ytaught was she with alle:

She leet no morsel from hir lippes falle,

Ne wette hir fyngres in hir sauce depe;

130   Wel koude she carie a morsel, and wel kepe

That no drope ne fille upon hir brist.

In curteisie was set ful muche hir list.

Hire over-lippe wyped she so clene

That in hir coppe ther was no ferthyng sene

135   Of grece, whan she dronken hadde hir draughte.

Ful semely after hir mete she raughte.

And sikerly, she was of greet desport,

And ful plesaunt, and amyable of port,

And peyned hir to countrefete cheere

140   Of court, and been estatlich of manere,

And to ben holden digne of reverence.

But, for to speken of hir conscience,

She was so charitable and so pitous

She wolde wepe, if that she saugh a mous

145   Kaught in a trappe, if it were deed or bledde.

Of smale houndes hadde she, that she fedde

With rosted flessh, or milk and wastel-breed.

But soore weep she if oon of hem were deed,

Or if men smoot it with a yerde smerte;

150   And al was conscience, and tendre herte.

Ful semyly hir wympul pynched was,

Hire nose tretys, hir eyen greye as glas,

Hir mouth ful smal, and therto softe and reed;

She sang the divine service beautifully,

Intoning through her nose, most becomingly,

And she spoke French elegantly and fluently,

125 *As taught by the school of Stratford-at-the-Bow,*

But she did not know French as spoken in Paris.

Moreover, at table she had been well taught:

And never let any morsel fall from her lips,

Nor did she dip her fingers deep into the sauce;

130 *She took care when carrying a morsel to her mouth*

So that no drop ever fell onto her breast.

Good manners were her greatest delight.

Her upper lip was always wiped so clean

That in her cup, you couldn't see even a farthing

135 *Of grease, when she had drunk her draught.*

She reached for her food graciously.

And certainly, she was very amusing company,

She was very pleasant and affable of bearing,

And she was at pains to imitate the outward appearance

140 *Of courtliness, and being of a noble sort,*

And would be held worthy of reverence.

But, to say something of her moral sense,

She was so charitable and compassionate

That she would weep if she saw a mouse

145 *Caught in a trap, if it were dead or bleeding.*

She had some little dogs, too, that she fed

With roast meat, or milk and fine white bread.

But she'd weep sorely if one of them died,

Or if men struck it with a painful stick;

150 *For her, all was feelings and being tender-hearted.*

Her pleated wimple was very seemly,

Her nose was fine; her eyes were grey as glass,

Her mouth was small and therewith soft and red;

But sikerly she hadde a fair forheed;

155 It was almoost a spanne brood, I trowe;

For, hardily, she was nat undergrowe.

Ful fetys was hir cloke, as I was war;

Of smal coral aboute hir arm she bar

A peire of bedes, gauded al with grene,

160 An theron heng a brooch of gold ful sheene,

On which ther was first write a crowned A,

And after *Amor vincit omnia.*

Another NONNE with hir hadde she,

That was hire chapeleyne, and preestes thre.

165 A MONK ther was, a fair for the maistrie,

An outridere, that lovede venerie,

A manly man, to been an abbot able.

Ful many a deyntee hors hadde he in stable,

And whan he rood, men myghte his brydel heere

170 Gynglen in a whistlynge wynd als cleere

And eek as loude, as dooth the chapel belle.

Ther as this lord was keper of the celle,

The reule of Seint Maure, or of Seint Beneit,

By cause that it was old and somdel streit

175 This ilke Monk leet olde thynges pace,

And heeld after the newe world the space.

He yaf nat of that text a pulled hen,

That seith that hunters beth nat hooly men,

Ne that a monk, whan he is recchelees,

180 Is likned til a fissh that is waterlees,-

This is to seyn, a monk out of his cloystre

But thilke text heeld he nat worth an oystre;

And I seyde his opinioun was good.

But certainly she had an attractive forehead;

155   *I think it was almost a full hand's breadth;*

For, truth to tell, she was not short.

I was mindful that her cloak was very elegant;

She wore a small coral about her arm

A set of green coloured beads,

160   *And thereon hung a brooch of shiny gold,*

On which was, firstly written a crowned A,

And underneath, "Love conquers all".

She had another NUN with her,

Who was her secretary; and three priests.

165   *A MONK there was, who was highly accomplished,*

Who worked outside the monastery, and who loved hunting,

A manly man, who was capable of becoming an abbot.

In his stable he had many fine horses,

And when he rode men might hear his bridle

170   *A-jingling in the whistling wind as clear*

And also as loud as is the chapel bell.

There, as this lord was Prior of the cell,

The rule of Saint Maurus or of Saint Benedict,

Because it was old and partly quite strict

175   *This self-same monk [would] leave such old things aside,*

And followed new-world customs instead.

He did not give a plucked hen for that book,

Which holds that hunters are not holy men,

Nor that a monk, when he does not heed the rules,

180   *Is likened to a fish that's out of wate,-*

That is to say, a monk outside of his cloister.

But he thought that text was not worth an oyster;

And I said his opinion was good.

What sholde he studie, and make hymselven wood,

185 Upon a book in cloystre alwey to poure,

Or swynken with his handes and laboure,

As Austyn bit? How shal the world be served?

Lat Austyn have his swynk to him reserved!

Therfore he was a prikasour aright:

190 Grehoundes he hadde, as swift as fowel in flight;

Of prikyng and of huntyng for the hare

Was al his lust, for no cost wolde he spare.

I seigh his sleves purfiled at the hond

With grys, and that the fyneste of a lond;

195 And, for to festne his hood under his chyn,

He hadde of gold ywroght a curious pyn;

A love-knotte in the gretter ende ther was.

His heed was balled, that shoon as any glas,

And eek his face, as it hadde been enoynt.

200 He was a lord ful fat and in good poynt,

Hise eyen stepe, and rollynge in his heed,

That stemed as a forneys of a leed;

His bootes souple, his hors in greet estaat.

Now certeinly he was a fair prelaat;

205 He was nat pale as a forpyned goost.

A fat swan loved he best of any roost.

His palfrey was as broun as is a berye,

A FRERE ther was, a wantowne and a merye,

A lymytour, a ful solempne man.

210 In alle the ordres foure is noon that kan

So muchel of daliaunce and fair langage.

He hadde maad ful many a mariage

Of yonge wommen at his owene cost.

Unto his ordre he was a noble post,

13

Why should he study and make himself go mad,
185   *Always reading books intently within the cloister,*
Or work with his hands and and labour,
As Augustine bids? How shall the world be thus served?
Let this work be kept for Augustine!
Therefore he was rightly a mounted huntsman:
190   *He had greyhounds, as swift as birds in flight;*
Since riding and hunting hares
Was his passion, for which he would spare no cost.
I saw his sleeves were lined at the hand
With grey fur, the finest in the land;
195   *Also, to fasten his hood beneath his chin,*
He had gold worked into an elaborate pin;
There was a love-knot in the larger end.
His head was bald and shone like any glass,
And also his face, as if it had been anointed with oil.
200   *He was a very fat lord, but was in good condition.*
His bulging eyes rolled about in his head,
That glowed like a fire beneath a cauldron;
His boots were supple; his horse was in fine condition.
Now certainly, he was a fine-looking church dignitary:
205   *He was not pale like some poor wasted ghost.*
He loved a fat swan the best of any roast.
His saddle horse was as brown as a berry.

There was a FRIAR, an extravagant and a merry one,
A licensed friar-beggar, a very important man.
210   *In all the Four Orders there is none that knew*
So much about sociability and elegant language.
He had arranged full many a marriage
Of women young, and this at his own cost.
He was a noble supporter of his order,

215	And wel biloved and famulier was he
	With frankeleyns overal in his contree,
	And eek with worthy wommen of the toun;
	For he hadde power of confessioun,
	As seyde hymself, moore than a curat,
220	For of his ordre he was licenciat.
	Ful swetely herde he confessioun,
	And plesaunt was his absolucioun:
	He was an esy man to yeve penaunce,
	Ther as he wiste to have a good pitaunce.
225	For unto a povre ordre for to yive
	Is signe that a man is wel yshryve;
	For, if he yaf, he dorste make avaunt,
	He wiste that a man was repentaunt;
	For many a man so harde is of his herte,
230	He may nat wepe, al thogh hym soore smerte;
	Therfore in stede of wepynge and preyeres
	Men moote yeve silver to the povre freres.
	His typet was ay farsed ful of knyves
	And pynnes, for to yeven yonge wyves.
235	And certeinly he hadde a murye note:
	Wel koude he synge, and pleyen on a rote;
	Of yeddynges he baar outrely the pris.
	His nekke whit was as the flour-de-lys;
	Therto he strong was as a champioun.
240	He knew the tavernes wel in every toun
	And everich hostiler and tappestere
	Bet than a lazar or a beggestere;
	For unto swich a worthy man as he
	Acorded nat, as by his facultee,
245	To have with sike lazars aqueyntaunce.
	It is nat honeste, it may nat avaunce,

215   *Well liked by all and he was sociable*
        With landowners everywhere in his district,
        And also with the worthy women of the town;
        For he had the power of hearing confession,
        As he himself said, more than a curate,
220   *For he was fully licensed by his order.*
        He heard confession very patiently,
        And his absolution was pleasant:
        He was lenient when giving penance,
        Then he knew he would receive a good gift.
225   *For to give money to an impoverished order*
        Signifies that any man has been fully confessed;
        For if one gave, the friar dared to boast,
        He knew that a man was repentant;
        For many a man is so hard of heart,
230   *He cannot weep even though he is in sore pain;*
        Therefore, instead of weeping and of prayers,
        Men might give silver to the poor friars.
        His hood was always full of knives
        And pins, to give to young wives.
235   *And certainly he had a merry voice:*
        He could sing well and play the hurdy-gurdy;
        But at reciting ballads he took the prize completely.
        His neck was as white as the lily flower;
        He was also strong as a champion.
240   *In towns he knew the taverns, every one*
        And every innkeeper and barmaid too
        Better than a leper or a beggar-woman;
        For unto such dignified man as he
        His professional experience taught it was not fitting,
245   *To have sick lepers as acquaintances.*
        It is not proper, and may not be profitable,

For to deelen with no swich poraille,

But al with riche and selleres of vitaille.

And over al, ther as profit sholde arise,

250 Curteis he was, and lowely of servyse.

Ther nas no man nowher so vertuous.

He was the beste beggere in his hous;

(And yaf a certeyn ferme for the graunt

Noon of his brethren cam ther in his haunt;)

255 For thogh a wydwe hadde noght a sho,

So plesaunt was his *"In principio"*

Yet wolde he have a ferthyng, er he wente;

His purchas was wel bettre than his rente.

And rage he koude, as it were right a whelp.

260 In love-dayes ther koude he muchel help,

For there he was nat lyk a cloysterer

With a thredbare cope, as is a povre scoler,

But he was lyk a maister or a pope;

Of double worstede was his semycope,

265 That rounded as a belle out of the presse.

Somwhat he lipsed for his wantownesse

To make his Englissh sweete upon his tonge;

And in his harpyng, whan that he hadde songe,

Hise eyen twynkled in his heed aryght

270 As doon the sterres in the frosty nyght.

This worthy lymytour was cleped Huberd.

A MARCHANT was ther with a forked berd,

In mottelee, and hye on horse he sat;

Upon his heed a Flaundryssh bever hat,

275 His bootes clasped faire and fetisly.

His resons he spak ful solempnely,

Sownynge alway th'encrees of his wynnyng.

To deal with such poor people,

But only with the rich and sellers of victuals.

So that profit should arise everywhere,

250 *He was courteous and humble.*

There was no other man so virtuous.

He was the finest beggar of his house;

(And gave a fee for being granted begging rights

So that none of his brethren dared enter his territory;)

255 *For though a widow had no shoes,*

His 'In the beginning', was so pleasant

He always got a farthing before he went;

His profits were always better than his proper income.

And he could frolic as if he was a puppy.

260 *On settling days he could be of great help,*

For he was not like a monk in cloisters

With threadbare cope like a poor scholar,

But he was like a teacher or like a pope;

Of double worsted was his short cloak,

265 *That was as round as a bell after being pressed.*

He lisped a little, out of affectation

To make his English pleasing upon his tongue;

And in his harping, after he had sung,

His two eyes twinkled in his head exactly

270 *Like the stars on a frosty night.*

This worthy district friar was called Hubert.

There was a MERCHANT with forked beard,

Wearing coloured cloth he sat high on his horse;

Upon his head there was a Flemish beaver hat,

275 *His boots were fastened attractively and elegantly.*

His spoke his opinions in a very grave manner,

Always speaking about his increasing profits.

He wolde the see were kept for any thyng

Bitwixe Middelburgh and Orewelle.

280   Wel koude he in eschaunge sheeldes selle.

This worthy man ful wel his wit bisette;

Ther wiste no wight that he was in dette,

So estatly was he of his governaunce

With his bargaynes and with his chevyssaunce.

285   For sothe, he was a worthy man with-alle,

But, sooth to seyn, I noot how men hym calle.

A CLERK ther was of Oxenford also,

That unto logyk hadde longe ygo.

As leene was his hors as is a rake,

290   And he nas nat right fat, I undertake,

But looked holwe and therto sobrely.

Ful thredbare was his overeste courtepy;

For he hadde geten hym yet no benefice,

Ne was so worldly for to have office.

295   For hym was levere have at his beddes heed

Twenty bookes, clad in blak or reed,

Of Aristotle and his philosophie,

Than robes riche, or fithele, or gay sautrie.

But al be that he was a philosophre,

300   Yet hadde he but litel gold in cofre;

But al that he myghte of his freendes hente,

On bookes and on lernynge he it spente,

And bisily gan for the soules preye

Of hem that yaf hym wherwith to scoleye.

305   Of studie took he moost cure and moost heede.

Noght o word spak he moore than was neede,

And that was seyd in forme and reverence,

And short and quyk, and ful of hy sentence;

He wanted the sea to be protected for business

Between Middelburgh in Holland and Orwell in England.

280   He was skilled at dealing in foreign currencies.

This worthy man employed his mind with great skill;

There, no person knew he was in debt,

So masterfully was he in conducting

His business transactions and his financial dealings.

285   Indeed, he was in truth a worthy man,

But, truth to tell, I cannot recall his name.

A CLERK [a scholar] from Oxford was also with us,

Who had turned to studying logic, long ago.

His horse was as lean as a rake,

290   I declare that he was not very fat,

But looked gaunt and thereby abstemious.

His overcoat was very threadbare;

For he had not yet gained an ecclesiastical living,

Nor was he sufficiently worldly to gain secular employment.

295   For he would rather have at his bed's head

Twenty books, all bound in black or red,

About Aristotle and his philosophy

Than splendid gowns, or a fiddle, or elegant psaltery.

But he was a philosopher above all,

300   He had but little gold in his coffers;

But all that he might borrow from his friends,

Was spent on books and on learning,

And then he'd pray diligently for those souls

Who gave him the wherewithal for his studies.

305   Of study he took the utmost care and most heed.

He did not speak one word more than was needed,

And that was said with great respect,

And short and quick and full of high meaning;

Sownynge in moral vertu was his speche,

310   And gladly wolde he lerne, and gladly teche.

A SERGEANT OF THE LAWE, war and wys,

That often hadde been at the Parvys,

Ther was also, ful riche of excellence.

Discreet he was, and of greet reverence-

315   He semed swich, hise wordes weren so wise.

Justice he was ful often in assise,

By patente, and by pleyn commissioun.

For his science, and for his heigh renoun,

Of fees and robes hadde he many oon.

320   So greet a purchasour was nowher noon:

Al was fee symple to hym in effect,

His purchasyng myghte nat been infect.

Nowher so bisy a man as he ther nas,

And yet he semed bisier than he was.

325   In termes hadde he caas and doomes alle

That from the tyme of Kyng William were falle.

Therto he koude endite and make a thyng,

Ther koude no wight pynche at his writyng;

And every statut koude he pleyn by rote.

330   He rood but hoomly in a medlee cote

Girt with a ceint of silk, with barres smale;

Of his array telle I no lenger tale.

A FRANKELEYN was in his compaignye.

Whit was his berd as is a dayesye;

335   Of his complexioun he was sangwyn.

Wel loved he by the morwe a sope in wyn,;

To lyven in delit was evere his wone,

For he was Epicurus owene sone,

His speech resounded with moral virtue,
310   *And gladly would he learn and gladly teach.*

A SERGEANT OF THE LAW, prudent and wise,
Who'd often advised at the porch at St Paul's,
Was also with us, a man of excellent qualities.
He was discreet, and greatly respected-
315   *For he seemed to be such, his words were so wise.*
He often sat as justice in the court of assizes,
With full authority granted by royal patent.
Because of his learning and his high renown,
Of fee income and robes he had many for himself.
320   *So great a land-purchaser was never known:*
In effect, acquiring land unconditionally was everything to him,
Wherefore his acquisitions of property could not be challenged.
There was not a man anywhere as busy as he,
And yet he seemed much busier than he was.
325   *He has all cases and all judgments*
That had occurred from King William's time.
And he could draft a document,
[About which] no person could quibble with his writing;
And he could recite every statute from his memory.
330   *He rode but badly in a medley coat*
Belted in a silken sash, with small stripes;
But of his dress I can talk no longer.

There was a FRANKLIN in his company.
His beard was as white as a daisy;
335   *His ruddy face showed his over-indulgences.*
He loved right well his morning bread dipped in wine.
Delightful living was always his goal,
For he was Epicurus' own son,

22

That heeld opinioun that pleyn delit

340 Was verray felicitee parfit.

An housholdere, and that a greet, was he;

Seint Julian was he in his contree.

His breed, his ale, was alweys after oon,

A bettre envyned man was nowher noon.

345 Withoute bake mete was nevere his hous

Of fissh and flessh, and that so plentevous,

It snewed in his hous of mete and drynke,

Of alle deyntees that men koude thynke.

After the sondry sesons of the yeer,

350 So chaunged he his mete and his soper.

Ful many a fat partrich hadde he in muwe,

And many a breem and many a luce in stuwe.

Wo was his cook, but if his sauce were

Poynaunt and sharp, and redy al his geere.

355 His table dormant in his halle alway

Stood redy covered al the longe day.

At sessiouns ther was he lord and sire;

Ful ofte tyme he was knyght of the shire.

An anlaas and a gipser al of silk

360 Heeng at his girdel, whit as morne milk.

A shirreve hadde he been, and a countour.

Was nowher swich a worthy vavasour.

An HABERDASSHERE and a CARPENTER,

A WEBBE, a DYERE, and a TAPYCER,-

365 And they were clothed alle in o lyveree

Of a solempne and a greet fraternitee.

Ful fressh and newe hir geere apiked was;

Hir knyves were chaped noght with bras,

But al with silver; wroght ful clene and weel,

Who held the opinion that full pleasure

340   *Meant complete and perfect happiness.*

He was a great householder;

Who had the hospitality of Saint Julian in his district.

His bread and ale were always similarly good

There was no man known with with fuller cellars.

345   *Baked meat pies were never lacking in his house*

Of fish and flesh, and that so plentiful,

His house seemed to snow with both food and drink,

Of all the dainties that a man could imagine.

According to the season of the year,

350   *So he could vary his midday meal and his supper.*

He kept many fattened partridges in pens,

And many bream and pike in fish-ponds.

Woe was his cook, if his sauces were not

Hot spiced and sharp, and he wasn't ready with his equipment.

355   *His fixed table, was always in his hall*

Standing set and covered throughout the whole day.

At county sessions was he presided as lord and sire;

And he was often a Knight of the Shire in parliament.

A dagger and a trinket-bag of silk

360   *Hung from his girdle, white as morning milk.*

He had been sheriff and a tax auditor.

And nowhere was there such a worthier landowner.

A HABERDASHER and a CARPENTER,

A WEAVER, a DYER, and a ARRAS-MAKER,-

365   *Were with us, all clothed in the same livery*

Of a great and distinguished guild.

Their gear was freshly and newly adorned;

Their weapons were not cheaply trimmed with brass,

But all with silver; made elegantly and well,

370   Hire girdles and hir pouches everydeel.

Wel semed ech of hem a fair burgeys

To sitten in a yeldehalle on a deys.

Everich, for the wisdom that he kan,

Was shaply for to been an alderman.

375   For catel hadde they ynogh and rente,

And eek hir wyves wolde it wel assente;

And elles certeyn, were they to blame.

It is ful fair to been ycleped "madame,"

And goon to vigilies al bifore,

380   And have a mantel roialliche ybore.

A COOK they hadde with hem for the nones

To boille the chiknes with the marybones,

And poudre-marchant tart, and galyngale.

Wel koude he knowe a draughte of London ale.

385   He koude rooste, and sethe, and broille, and frye,

Maken mortreux, and wel bake a pye.

But greet harm was it, as it thoughte me,

That on his shyne a mormal hadde he.

For blankmanger, that made he with the beste.

390   A SHIPMAN was ther, wonynge fer by weste;

For aught I woot, he was of Dertemouthe.

He rood upon a rouncy, as he kouthe,

In a gowne of faldyng to the knee.

A daggere hangynge on a laas hadde he

395   Aboute his nekke, under his arm adoun.

The hoote somer hadde maad his hewe al broun,

And certeinly he was a good felawe.

Ful many a draughte of wyn had he ydrawe

Fro Burdeux-ward, whil that the chapman sleep.

370   *Their girdles and their pouches, everything.*

    Each man of them seemed to be a very upright citizen

    To sit in the guildhall on a dais.

    And each of them, for the wisdom he knew,

    [Made him] well-suited to be an alderman.

375   *For chattels and income they had plenty,*

    And of which their wives would also approve;

    Or else they would certainly be held to blame.

    [For] it is splendid to be called "my lady,"

    And to lead the procession at feasts on the eve of holidays,

380   *And have one's train carried in a royal manner.*

    They had a COOK with them for the occasion

    To boil the chickens with the marrow-bones,

    And flavoured tartly and galangal.

    He could easily recognise a draught of London ale.

385   *He could roast and boil and broil and fry,*

    Make hearty soup, and well-bake a pie.

    But it was a great pity, it seemed to me,

    That he had a weeping ulcer on his shin.

    For sweet blanc-mange, he ranked amongst the best.

390   *There was a SHIPMAN, living far out west;*

    For all I know, he was from Dartmouth.

    He sadly rode a cart horse, to the best he could,

    In a gown of rough cloth that reached to his knee.

    He had a dagger hanging on a strap

395   *Around his neck, and down under his arm.*

    The summer's heat had made him brown in colour,

    And certainly he was a good fellow.

    He had drawn very many drafts of wine

    From Bordeaux, while the merchant was asleep.

400	Of nyce conscience took he no keep.
	If that he faught, and hadde the hyer hond,
	By water he sente hem hoom to every lond.
	But of his craft, to rekene wel his tydes,
	His stremes, and his daungers hym bisides,
405	His herberwe and his moone, his lodemenage,
	Ther nas noon swich from Hulle to Cartage.
	Hardy he was, and wys to undertake;
	With many a tempest hadde his berd been shake.
	He knew alle the havenes as they were,
410	From Gootlond to the Cape of Fynystere,
	And every cryke in Britaigne and in Spayne.
	His barge ycleped was the Maudelayne.
	With us ther was a DOCTOUR OF PHISIK;
	In al this world ne was ther noon hym lik,
415	To speke of phisik and of surgerye,
	For he was grounded in astronomye.
	He kepte his pacient a ful greet deel
	In houres, by his magyk natureel.
	Wel koude he fortunen the ascendent
420	Of his ymages for his pacient.
	He knew the cause of everich maladye,
	Were it of hoot, or coold, or moyste, or drye,
	And where they engendred, and of what humour.
	He was a verray parfit praktisour:
425	The cause yknowe, and of his harm the roote,
	Anon he yaf the sike man his boote.
	Ful redy hadde he hise apothecaries
	To sende him drogges and his letuaries,
	For ech of hem made oother for to wynne-
430	Hir frendshipe nas nat newe to bigynne.

400   *He did not keep with having a good conscience.*

If he fought and won the upper hand,

By water he'd send them home to every land [by walking the plank].

But of his sea-faring skills, he was good at reckoning the tides,

His currents and the dangers nearby,

405   *His harbours, and the moon's positions, his pilotage,*

There was no one better from Hull to Carthage.

He was brave, and undertook things prudently;

His beard been shaken by many tempests.

He knew where all the safe harbours were,

410   *From Gotland to the Cape of Finisterre,*

And every creek and estuary in Brittany and Spain.

His vessel was called the Maudelayne.

With us there was a DOCTOR OF MEDICINE;

In all this world was no other like him,

415   *To speak of medicine and surgery,*

For he was well-instructed in astronomy.

He took very great care of his patients

By horoscopes and by his natural science.

He could accurately calculate the planets' positions

420   *For the astronomical talismans he used for his patients.*

He knew the cause of every illness,

Were it of hot or cold, or moist or dry,

And where they procreated, and by what bodily humour.

He was a very good practitioner:

425   *He knew the cause of illness, to the deepest root,*

He gave to the sick man his remedy straight away.

His apothecaries were fully ready

To send him drugs and his medicines,

For each of them made profit for the other-

430   *Their friendship was not newly begun.*

Wel knew he the olde Esculapius,

And Deyscorides and eek Rufus,

Olde Ypocras, Haly, and Galyen,

Serapioun, Razis, and Avycen,

435   Averrois, Damascien, and Constantyn,

Bernard, and Gatesden, and Gilbertyn.

Of his diete mesurable was he,

For it was of no superfluitee,

But of greet norissyng, and digestible.

440   His studie was but litel on the Bible.

In sangwyn and in pers he clad was al,

Lyned with taffata and with sendal;

And yet he was but esy of dispence;

He kepte that he wan in pestilence.

445   For gold in phisik is a cordial,

Therfore he lovede gold in special.

A good WIF was ther, OF biside BATHE,

But she was somdel deef, and that was scathe.

Of clooth-makyng she hadde swich an haunt,

450   She passed hem of Ypres and of Gaunt.

In al the parisshe wif ne was ther noon

That to the offrynge bifore hire sholde goon;

And if ther dide, certeyn so wrooth was she,

That she was out of alle charitee.

455   Hir coverchiefs ful fyne weren of ground;

I dorste swere they weyeden ten pound

That on a Sonday weren upon hir heed.

Hir hosen weren of fyn scarlet reed,

Ful streite yteyd, and shoes ful moyste and newe.

460   Boold was hir face, and fair, and reed of hewe.

She was a worthy womman al hir lyve:

He was well read in old Æsculapius,

And Dioscorides, and also Rufus,

Old Hippocrates, and Hali, and Galen,

Serapion, Rhazes, and Avicen,

435   Averrhoes, John Damascene and Constantine,

Bernard and Gaddesden, and Gilbert.

In his diet he was measured,

For it had nothing in excess,

But was greatly nourishing and digestible.

440   But he had read little of the Bible.

He was clothed all over in blue and scarlet,

Lined with a taffeta and with silk;

And yet he was moderate his expenses;

He kept the gold he gained from times of plague.

445   For gold in medicine is a fine stimulant for the heart,

Therefore he loved gold in particular.

There was a HOUSEWIFE come from near BATH,

But it was a shame that she was somewhat deaf.

At making cloth she had such skill,

450   She bettered those of Ypres and of Ghent.

In all the parish there was no wife

Who should go to make an offering before her;

And if one did, indeed, she was very angry,

That it put her out of all her charity.

455   Her kerchiefs were made from fabric of the finest weave;

I dare swear that they weighed ten pounds

Which, on a Sunday, she wore on her head.

Her stockings were of fine scarlet red,

Close gartered, and her shoes were very supple and new.

460   Her face was strong and attractive, and was red in colour.

he'd been respectable throughout her life:

30

Housbondes at chirche dore she hadde fyve,

Withouthen oother compaignye in youthe, -

But therof nedeth nat to speke as nowthe.

465 And thries hadde she been at Jerusalem;

She hadde passed many a straunge strem;

At Rome she hadde been, and at Boloigne,

In Galice at Seint-Jame, and at Coloigne.

She koude muchel of wandrynge by the weye.

470 Gat-tothed was she, soothly for to seye.

Upon an amblere esily she sat,

Ywympled wel, and on hir heed an hat

As brood as is a bokeler or a targe;

A foot-mantel aboute hir hipes large,

475 And on hir feet a paire of spores sharpe.

In felaweshipe wel koude she laughe and carpe.

Of remedies of love she knew per chaunce,

For she koude of that art the olde daunce.

A good man was ther of religioun,

480 And was a povre PERSOUN OF A TOUN,

But riche he was of hooly thoght and werk.

He was also a lerned man, a clerk,

That Cristes gospel trewely wolde preche;

His parisshens devoutly wolde he teche.

485 Benynge he was, and wonder diligent,

And in adversitee ful pacient,

And swich he was ypreved ofte sithes.

Ful looth were hym to cursen for his tithes,

But rather wolde he yeven, out of doute,

490 Unto his povre parisshens aboute

Of his offryng and eek of his substaunce.

He koude in litel thyng have suffisaunce.

With five husbands married at the church door,

Not counting other company in her youth, -

But thereof there's no need to speak of that now.

465 *And she had journeyed to Jerusalem three times;*

She had crossed many a foreign sea;

She had been at Rome, and at Boulogne,

In Galicia, at St James of Compostella, and at Cologne.

She knew a great deal about travelling around.

470 *Gap-toothed was she, truth to tell.*

She sat easily upon an ambling horse,

She wore a large wimple, and a hat upon her head

As broad as is a buckler or a shield;

A rug was wrapped around her large hips,

475 *And on her feet a pair of sharpened spurs.*

In company well could she laugh and complain.

The remedies of love she knew, by chance,

For she knew all the tricks of that old trade.

There was a good man of religion,

480 *And was a poor PARSON OF A TOWN,*

But rich he was in holy thought and work.

He was a learned man also, a scholar,

Who preached Christ's own gospel truly;

He would devoutly teach his parishioners.

485 *Gracious was he and extremely diligent,*

And was very patient in adverse times,

And for which he was often proven.

He was loath to excommunicate for not paying tithes,

But rather would he give, in case of doubt,

490 *Unto his poor parishioners in the vicinity*

Part of the offerings and also some of his own income.

He knew how to to make a sufficiency out of a few things.

Wyd was his parisshe, and houses fer asonder,

But he ne lefte nat, for reyn ne thonder,

495   In siknesse nor in meschief to visite

The ferreste in his parisshe, muche and lite,

Upon his feet, and in his hand a staf.

This noble ensample to his sheep he yaf,

That first he wroghte, and afterward he taughte.

500   Out of the gosple he tho wordes caughte,

And this figure he added eek therto,

That if gold ruste, what shal iren do?

For if a preest be foul, on whom we truste,

No wonder is a lewed man to ruste;

505   And shame it is, if a prest take keep,

A shiten shepherde and a clene sheep.

Wel oghte a preest ensample for to yive,

By his clennesse, how that his sheep sholde lyve.

He sette nat his benefice to hyre

510   And leet his sheep encombred in the myre

And ran to Londoun unto Seinte Poules

To seken hym a chaunterie for soules,

Or with a bretherhed to been witholde;

But dwelt at hoom, and kepte wel his folde,

515   So that the wolf ne made it nat myscarie;

He was a shepherde and noght a mercenarie.

And though he hooly were and vertuous,

He was to synful men nat despitous,

Ne of his speche daungerous ne digne,

520   But in his techyng discreet and benygne;

To drawen folk to hevene by fairnesse,

By good ensample, this was his bisynesse.

But it were any persone obstinat,

What so he were, of heigh or lough estat,

His parish was large, and with houses far apart,

But never did he fail, in rain or thunder,

495   To visit in sickness, or in misfortune

Those living the furthest, whether high or low ranking,

Going by foot, and with a staff in his hand.

He set a very fine example to his flock,

That first he worked and afterwards he taught.

500   His words were taken out of the gospel,

And he added this metaphor thereunto,

That, if gold rust, what shall iron do?

For if the priest be foul, in whom we trust,

It is no wonder that an ignorant man will decay;

505   And it is a shame, if, as every priest should take heed,

A dung-stained shepherd tends clean sheep.

Well ought a priest to set an example,

By his own purity, how his flock should live.

He never let his benefice for hire

510   Leaving his flock to flounder in the mire

And ran off to London, up to Saint Paul's

To become a chantry priest singing for wealthy dead souls,

Nor to be hired as a chaplain to a guild;

But dwelt at home and looked after his fold,

515   That no wolf could make his plans miscarry;

He was a shepherd and not mercenary.

And although he was holy and virtuous,

To sinners he was not scornful,

Nor was he haughty in his speech, nor threatening,

520   But in his teaching respectful and kind;

To lead folk into heaven by gentleness,

By his good example, this was his business.

But if some sinful person proved obstinate,

Be whoever they were, [whether] of high or low rank,

525	Hym wolde he snybben sharply for the nonys.
	A bettre preest I trowe, that nowher noon ys.
	He waited after no pompe and reverence,
	Ne maked him a spiced conscience,
	But Cristes loore, and Hise apostles twelve
530	He taughte, but first he folwed it hymselve.

	With hym ther was a PLOWMAN, was his brother,
	That hadde ylad of dong ful many a fother;
	A trewe swynkere and a good was he,
	Lyvynge in pees and parfit charitee.
535	God loved he best with al his hoole herte
	At alle tymes, thogh him gamed or smerte,
	And thanne his neighebor right as hym-selve.
	He wolde thresshe, and therto dyke and delve,
	For Cristes sake, for every povre wight
540	Withouten hire, if it lay in his myght.
	Hise tithes payed he ful faire and wel,
	Bothe of his propre swynk and his catel.
	In a tabard he rood, upon a mere.

	Ther was also a REVE and a MILLERE,
545	A SOMNOUR and a PARDONER also,
	A MAUNCIPLE, and myself - ther were namo.

	The MILLERE was a stout carl for the nones;
	Ful byg he was of brawn and eek of bones-
	That proved wel, for over al ther he cam
550	At wrastlynge he wolde have alwey the ram.
	He was short-sholdred, brood, a thikke knarre,
	Ther was no dore that he nolde heve of harre,
	Or breke it at a rennyng with his heed.

525 *He would reproach him sharply.*

I believe there is no better priest anywhere.

He had no appetite for pomp or reverence,

Nor possessed a fastidious conscience,

But as to Christ's teachings, and His twelve apostles

530 *He taught, but first he followed it himself.*

With him there was a PLOWMAN, who was his brother,

That had hauled many a load of dung;

For a good and true worker was he,

Living in peace and perfect charity.

535 *He loved God best, and that with his whole heart*

At all times, though it pleased or hurt him,

And thereby he loved his neighbour, like himself.

He would thresh and also make ditches and dig,

For Christ's own sake, for every poor person

540 *All without pay, if it was in his ability to do so.*

He paid his taxes, fully and fairly,

Both by his own toil and by the things he'd sell.

He rode upon a mare wearing a sleeveless jacket.

There were also a REEVE and MILLER,

545 *A SUMMONER, and also a PARDONER,*

A MANCIPLE and myself - there were no more.

The MILLER was indeed a stout fellow;

Hardy and big of muscle and also of bone-

Which was well proved, for wherever he came

550 *He always took the prize at wrestling.*

He had a short, thick neck, was broad, a stocky fellow,

There was no door that he couldn't heave from its hinges,

Or break through it, by running at it with his head.

His berd as any sowe or fox was reed,

555 And therto brood, as though it were a spade.

Upon the cop right of his nose he hade

A werte, and thereon stood a toft of herys,

Reed as the brustles of a sowes erys;

Hise nosethirles blake were and wyde.

560 A swerd and bokeler bar he by his syde.

His mouth as greet was as a greet forneys.

He was a janglere and a goliardeys,

And that was moost of synne and harlotries.

Wel koude he stelen corn, and tollen thries;

565 And yet he hadde a thombe of gold, pardee.

A whit cote and a blew hood wered he.

A baggepipe wel koude he blowe and sowne,

And therwithal he broghte us out of towne.

A gentil MAUNCIPLE was ther of a temple,

570 Of which achatours myghte take exemple

For to be wise in byynge of vitaille;

For wheither that he payde or took by taille,

Algate he wayted so in his achaat

That he was ay biforn, and in good staat.

575 Now is nat that of God a ful fair grace,

That swich a lewed mannes wit shal pace

The wisdom of an heep of lerned men?

Of maistres hadde he mo than thries ten,

That weren of lawe expert and curious,

580 Of whiche ther weren a duszeyne in that hous

Worthy to been stywardes of rente and lond

Of any lord that is in Engelond,

To maken hym lyve by his propre good,

In honour dettelees (but if he were wood),

His beard was red like any sow or fox,

555   *And it was broad, like a spade.*

Upon the top of his nose he had

A wart, and thereon stood a tuft of hairs,

As red as the bristles in a sow's ears;

His nostrils they were black and very wide.

560   *A sword and buckler bore he by his side.*

His mouth was as big as a large furnace.

He was a idle-talker and a joker,

And that was mostly about sin and sexual misconduct.

He knew how to steal corn and charge fees three times over;

565   *And yet, by God, he had a thumb of gold.*

He wore a white coat and blue hood.

A bagpipe he could blow and play very well,

And with which he brought us out of town.

There was a noble MANCIPLE [provisions buyer] of the Inner Temple,

570   *To whom all buyers might quite well resort*

To learn his art of buying food and drink;

For whether he paid cash or on credit,

Always he watched carefully for when to buy

That he was always ahead and in a good situation.

575   *Now is it not by God's fair grace,*

That such an uneducated man had the wit to outpace

The wisdom of a crowd of learned men?

He had more than thirty masters,

Who were expert and skilled in the law,

580   *Whereof there were a dozen in that house*

Fit to be stewards of both rent and land

Of any lord that is in in England,

To make his living by his own wealth,

In honour, debtless (unless he was crazy),

585   Or lyve as scarsly as hym list desire,

And able for to helpen al a shire

In any caas that myghte falle or happe-

And yet this Manciple sette hir aller cappe.

The REVE was a sclendre colerik man.

590   His berd was shave as ny as ever he kan;

His heer was by his erys ful round yshorn;

His top was dokked lyk a preest biforn.

Ful longe were his legges, and ful lene,

Ylyk a staf, ther was no calf ysene.

595   Wel koude he kepe a gerner and a bynne;

Ther was noon auditour koude on him wynne.

Wel wiste he by the droghte and by the reyn,

The yeldynge of his seed and of his greyn.

His lordes sheep, his neet, his dayerye,

600   His swyn, his hors, his stoor, and his pultrye,

Was hoolly in this Reves governynge,

And by his covenant yaf the rekenynge,

Syn that his lord was twenty yeer of age,

Ther koude no man brynge hym in arrerage.

605   Ther nas baillif, ne hierde, nor oother hyne,

That he ne knew his sleighte and his covyne;

They were adrad of hym as of the deeth.

His wonyng was ful faire upon an heeth;

With grene trees shadwed was his place.

610   He koude bettre than his lord purchace.

Ful riche he was astored pryvely:

His lord wel koude he plesen subtilly,

To yeve and lene hym of his owene good,

And have a thank, and yet a cote and hood.

615   In youthe he hadde lerned a good myster;

585   *Or live as frugally as he might desire,*

         These men were able to to help an entire county

         In any emergency that ever might befall-

         And yet this manciple outwitted them all.

         The REEVE he was a slender, choleric man.

590   *Who shaved his beard as close as he knew how;*

         His hair was cut round even around his ears;

         His top was cut short like a priest's.

         His legs were very long and very lean,

         And like a staff, with no calf to be seen.

595   *He knew well how to manage a granary and a storage bin;*

         No auditor could ever win by catching him out.

         He could foretell, by drought and by the rain,

         What his seed and his grain would yield.

         His lord's sheep and his oxen and his dairy cows,

600   *His swine and horses, all his stores, his poultry,*

         Was entirely within this steward's management,

         And, by agreement, he'd produced the accounts,

         Since his lord was twenty years old,

         Yet no man had ever found him in arrears.

605   *There was no agent, herdsman or other servant,*

         That he didn't know their cunning and deceit;

         They were as afraid of him as they were of the plague.

         His dwelling was well positioned on a heath;

         His house was shaded by green trees.

610   *He knew better than his lord about buying land.*

         He was very rich in his own private right:

         He knew very well how to subtly please his lord,

         By giving or lending to him some of his own goods,

         And received their thanks by being given coats and hoods.

615   *In youth he had learned a good trade;*

He was a wel good wrighte, a carpenter.

This Reve sat upon a ful good stot,

That was al pomely grey, and highte Scot.

A long surcote of pers upon he hade,

620 And by his syde he baar a rusty blade.

Of Northfolk was this Reve, of which I telle,

Bisyde a toun men clepen Baldeswelle.

Tukked he was as is a frere aboute,

And evere he rood the hyndreste of oure route.

625 A SOMONOUR was ther with us in that place,

That hadde a fyr-reed cherubynnes face,

For saucefleem he was, with eyen narwe.

As hoot he was and lecherous as a sparwe,

With scalled browes blake, and piled berd,

630 Of his visage children were aferd.

Ther nas quyk-silver, lytarge, ne brymstoon,

Boras, ceruce, ne oille of tartre noon,

Ne oynement, that wolde clense and byte,

That hym myghte helpen of his whelkes white,

635 Nor of the knobbes sittynge on his chekes.

Wel loved he garleek, oynons, and eek lekes,

And for to drynken strong wyn, reed as blood;

Thanne wolde he speke and crie as he were wood.

And whan that he wel dronken hadde the wyn,

640 Than wolde he speke no word but Latyn.

A fewe termes hadde he, two or thre,

That he had lerned out of som decree-

No wonder is, he herde it al the day,

And eek ye knowen wel how that a jay

645 Kan clepen "Watte" as wel as kan the pope.

But whoso koude in oother thyng hym grope,

He was a very good workman, a carpenter.

This Reeve sat upon a horse that could trot very well,

And was all dapple-grey, and was named Scot.

He wore a long outer coat of blue,

620   And at his side he bore a rusty blade.

This Reeve of whom I speak was from Norfolk,

From near a town that men call Bawdeswell.

He hitched up his coat like a friar,

And he always rode at the rear of our troop.

625   A SUMMONER was with us in that place,

Who had a fiery-red, cherub's face,

He was afflicted with eczema; his eyes were narrow.

He was as hot-blooded and lecherous as a sparrow,

With black and scabby brows and scanty beard,

630   He had a face that little children feared.

There was no mercury, sulphur, or brimstone,

Borax, ceruse, nor oil of tartar,

Nor ointment that would cleanse and consume,

To help rid him of those white pustules,

635   Nor of the large boils on his cheeks.

He greatly loved garlic, onions, and also leeks,

And drinking strong wine as red as blood;

Then would he talk and shout like a madman.

And when he had drunk a great deal of wine,

640   He would then utter no word except Latin.

He had learned some phrases, [maybe] two or three,

Which he had taught himself from some ecclesiastical text-

No wonder, for he had heard it all day,

And also you know how well even a jay

645   Knows how to call out "Walter" as well as the pope.

But whosoever could delve into what he knew about other things,

Thanne hadde he spent al his philosophie;

Ay *"Questio quid iuris"* wolde he crie.

He was a gentil harlot and a kynde;

650 A bettre felawe sholde men noght fynde;

He wolde suffre, for a quart of wyn,

A good felawe to have his concubyn

A twelf-monthe, and excuse hym atte fulle;

Ful prively a fynch eek koude he pulle.

655 And if he foond owher a good felawe,

He wolde techen him to have noon awe,

In swich caas, of the ercedekenes curs,

But if a mannes soule were in his purs;

For in his purs he sholde ypunysshed be.

660 "Purs is the erchedekenes helle," seyde he.

But wel I woot he lyed right in dede;

Of cursyng oghte ech gilty man him drede,

For curs wol slee, right as assoillyng savith,

And also war him of a *Significavit*.

665 In daunger hadde he at his owene gise

The yonge girles of the diocise,

And knew hir conseil, and was al hir reed.

A gerland hadde he set upon his heed

As greet as it were for an ale-stake;

670 A bokeleer hadde he maad him of a cake.

With hym ther rood a gentil PARDONER

Of Rouncivale, his freend and his compeer,

That streight was comen fro the court of Rome.

Ful loude he soong "Com hider, love, to me!"

675 This Somonour bar to hym a stif burdoun;

Was nevere trompe of half so greet a soun.

This Pardoner hadde heer as yelow as wex,

Then found he had used up his entire learning;

He would cry "The question is what point of law applies."

He was a noble rascal, and a kind one;

650 A better comrade would be hard to find;

For a quart of wine, he would let,

Some good fellow have his concubine

For twelve months, and forgive him completely;

But he could also pull off a secret trick [and continue having sex with her].

655 And if he chanced upon a good fellow,

He would teach him not to be afraid,

Of the archdeacon's curse of excommunication,

But if a man kept his soul inside his purse;

It was in his purse that he should be punished.

660 He said, "The purse is the archdeacon's Hell."

But know that he lied about what he said;

Every guilty man should dread excommunication,

For excommunication can kill, as absolution saves,

And be aware of the order for imprisonment.

665 He had in his own power had at his own pleasure

The young people in the diocese,

He knew all their secrets, and gave them his advice.

A garland he had set upon his head

As large as a sign outside a tavern;

670 He had made himself a shield made of bread.

With him there rode a noble PARDONER

Of Rouncival, his friend and his companion,

Who he had journeyed straight from the court of Rome.

He sang "Come hither, love, to me!" very loudly.

675 The summoner joined with his song in a deep bass;

There was no trumpet that made even half so great a sound.

This Pardoner's hair was as yellow as wax,

But smothe it heeng as dooth a strike of flex;

By ounces henge his lokkes that he hadde,

680 And therwith he hise shuldres overspradde;

But thynne it lay by colpons oon and oon.

But hood, for jolitee, wered he noon,

For it was trussed up in his walet.

Hym thoughte he rood al of the newe jet;

685 Dischevelee, save his cappe, he rood al bare.

Swiche glarynge eyen hadde he as an hare.

A vernycle hadde he sowed upon his cappe.

His walet lay biforn hym in his lappe

Bretful of pardoun come from Rome al hoot.

690 A voys he hadde as smal as hath a goot,

No berd hadde he, ne nevere sholde have;

As smothe it was as it were late shave,

I trowe he were a geldyng or a mare.

But of his craft, from Berwyk into Ware,

695 Ne was ther swich another pardoner;

For in his male he hadde a pilwe-beer,

Which that he seyde was Oure Lady veyl:

He seyde he hadde a gobet of the seyl

That Seint Peter hadde, whan that he wente

700 Upon the see, til Jesu Crist hym hente.

He hadde a croys of latoun ful of stones,

And in a glas he hadde pigges bones.

But with thise relikes, whan that he fond

A povre persoun dwellyng upon lond,

705 Upon a day he gat hym moore moneye

Than that the person gat in monthes tweye;

And thus, with feyned flaterye and japes,

He made the persoun and the peple his apes.

But trewely to tellen atte laste,

But it hung straightly like a hank of flax;

And such hair that he had hung like wisps,

680 Which he spread over his shoulders;

But they lay one by one in thin strands.

But he wore no hood to create a good appearance,

For it was packed up in his knapsack.

It seemed to him he went in the latest style;

685 Except for his cap, he went bare-headed with unbound hair.

He had glaring eyes just like a hare.

He had an image of Christ's face sewed on his cap.

On his lap, his knapsack lay before him

Stuffed full of pardons hot from Rome.

690 His voice was small like the bleating of a goat,

No beard had he, nor ever could have;

For his face was as smooth as if he had just shaved,

I think he was either a eunuch or a homosexual.

But in his cunning art, from Berwick unto Ware,

695 Never was there such a pardoner anywhere;

For in his bag he had a pillowcase,

Which, he said, was Our True Lady's veil:

He said he had a piece of the very sail

That good Saint Peter had, when he went

700 Upon the sea, until Jesus took him.

He had a cross made of brass set full of stones,

And in a bottle he had some pig's bones.

But with these relics, when he came upon

Some simple parson from the countryside,

705 He gained more money that one day

Than the parson earned in two months;

And thus, with false flattery and tricks,

He made fools of the parson and the congregation.

But to tell the whole truth at last,

710   He was in chirche a noble ecclesiaste.

Wel koude he rede a lessoun or a storie,

But alderbest he song an offertorie;

or wel he wiste, whan that song was songe,

He moste preche, and wel affile his tonge

715   To wynne silver, as he ful wel koude;

Therfore he song the murierly and loude.

Now have I toold you shortly in a clause,

Th'estaat, th'array, the nombre, and eek the cause

Why that assembled was this compaignye

720   In Southwerk, at this gentil hostelrye

That highte the Tabard, faste by the Belle.

But now is tyme to yow for to telle

How that we baren us that ilke nyght,

Whan we were in that hostelrie alyght;

725   And after wol I telle of our viage

And all the remenaunt of oure pilgrimage.

But first I pray yow, of youre curteisye,

That ye n'arette it nat my vileynye,

Thogh that I pleynly speke in this mateere,

730   To telle yow hir wordes and hir cheere,

Ne thogh I speke hir wordes proprely.

For this ye knowen also wel as I,

Whoso shal telle a tale after a man,

He moot reherce as ny as evere he kan

735   Everich a word, if it be in his charge,

Al speke he never so rudeliche or large,

Or ellis he moot telle his tale untrewe,

Or feyne thyng, or fynde wordes newe.

He may nat spare, al thogh he were his brother;

740   He moot as wel seye o word as another.

710   *He was, in church, a fine ecclesiast.*

         Who knew well how to read a lesson or a story,

         But he sang an offertory best of all;

         For well he knew when that song was sung,

         He must preach, and with his very polished tongue

715   *He could very well gain some silver;*

         Therefore he sang merrily and loudly.

         Now have I told you truthfully, in a brief statement,

         The state, the array, the number, and the cause

         As to why this company has assembled

720   *In Southwark, at this fine hostelry*

         Named the Tabard Inn, close by the Bell.

         But now the time is come to tell you

         How all we bore ourselves that night,

         When we arrived at the hostelry;

725   *And afterward I will tell you about our journey*

         And the remainder of our pilgrimage.

         But first, I pray you, as a matter of your courtesy,

         That you will not impute any rudeness on my part,

         If I speak plainly on this matter,

730   *To tell you of their words and their manner,*

         Although I speak their works exactly.

         For you know as well as I,

         Whosoever repeats a tale told by a man,

         He must repeat it, as nearly as he knows how

735   *Every least word, if it is in his power to do so,*

         However rude it be, or however freely,

         Or else he must tell his tale untruthfully,

         Or falsifying the thing, or finding new words.

         He may not spare the truth, even if were his brother;

740   *He must as well say one word as another.*

Crist spak hymself ful brode in hooly writ,

And, wel ye woot, no vileynye is it.

Eek Plato seith, whoso kan hym rede,

The wordes moote be cosyn to the dede.

745 Also I prey yow to foryeve it me,

Al have I nat set folk in hir degree

Heere in this tale, as that they sholde stonde.

My wit is short, ye may wel understonde.

Greet chiere made oure Hoost us everichon,

750 And to the soper sette he us anon.

He served us with vitaille at the beste;

Strong was the wyn, and wel to drynke us leste.

A semely man OURE HOOSTE was withalle

For to been a marchal in an halle.

755 A large man he was, with eyen stepe -

A fairer burgeys was ther noon in Chepe -

Boold of his speche, and wys, and well ytaught,

And of manhod hym lakkede right naught.

Eek therto he was right a myrie man,

760 And after soper pleyen he bigan,

And spak of myrthe amonges othere thynges,

Whan that we hadde maad our rekenynges,

And seyde thus: "Now lordynges, trewely,

Ye been to me right welcome hertely;

765 For by my trouthe, if that I shal nat lye,

I saugh nat this yeer so myrie a compaignye

Atones in this herberwe, as is now.

Fayn wolde I doon yow myrthe, wiste I how.

And of a myrthe I am right now bythoght,

770 To doon yow ese, and it shal coste noght.

Ye goon to Caunterbury - God yow speede,

Christ spoke very frankly, in the scriptures,

And, you know well, there's no shame in it.

Also Plato says, whosoever knows how to read him,

The words must be akin to the deed.

745 *Also, I pray that you'll forgive me,*

If I have not arranged folk, in their proper rank

Here in this tale, as where they should stand.

My wits are not the best, you'll understand.

Our host offered great entertainment to every one of us,

750 *And set us all to supper straight away.*

And served us with the best victuals;

Strong was the wine and pleasant for us to drink.

Indeed, OUR HOST was a very pleasing man

Fit to have been a master of ceremonies in a hall.

755 *He was a large man, with bulging eyes -*

No-one else in Cheapside was as fine a businessman -

Bold in his speech, and wise, and very well educated,

And as to manly qualities he lacked nothing.

Also, he was a very merry man,

760 *And after supper, he began to make play,*

Speaking of mirth among some other things,

When all of us had paid our bills,

And saying thus: "Now gentlemen, verily,

You are all heartily welcome here;

765 *For by my truth, and telling you no lie,*

I have not seen, this year, so merry a company

Here in this inn, as there is now.

I would be glad to make you happy, and I know how.

I have just this moment thought of a game,

770 *To give you joy, and it shall cost you nothing.*

"You go to Canterbury; may God speed you,

The blisful martir quite yow youre meede!

And wel I woot, as ye goon by the weye,

Ye shapen yow to talen and to pleye,

775 For trewely, confort ne myrthe is noon

To ride by the weye doumb as stoon;

And therfore wol I maken yow disport,

As I seyde erst, and doon yow som confort.

And if yow liketh alle by oon assent

780 For to stonden at my juggement,

And for to werken as I shal yow seye,

To-morwe, whan ye riden by the weye,

Now, by my fader soule that is deed,

But ye be myrie, I wol yeve yow myn heed!

785 Hoold up youre hond, withouten moore speche."

Oure conseil was nat longe for to seche.

Us thoughte it was noght worth to make it wys,

And graunted hym, withouten moore avys,

And bad him seye his voirdit, as hym leste.

790 "Lordynges," quod he, "now herkneth for the beste;

But taak it nought, I prey yow, in desdeyn.

This is the poynt, to speken short and pleyn,

That ech of yow, to shorte with oure weye,

In this viage shal telle tales tweye

795 To Caunterbury-ward I mene it so,

And homward he shal tellen othere two,

Of aventures that whilom han bifalle.

And which of yow that bereth hym best of alle,

That is to seyn, that telleth in this caas

800 Tales of best sentence and moost solaas,

Shal have a soper at oure aller cost

Heere in this place, sittynge by this post,

Whan that we come agayn fro Caunterbury.

And may the blessed martyr reward you!

And well I know, as you go on your way,

You'll tell tales to entertain yourselves,

775 *For truly there's no comfort or pleasure*

Riding the roads as dumb as a stone;

And therefore will I furnish you with a game,

As I just said, to give you some comfort.

And if you like, you agree unanimously

780 *To be ruled by my judgment,*

And to act as I shall say to you,

Tomorrow, when you ride upon your way,

Then, by my dead father's spirit,

If you're not merry, I'll give you my head!

785 *Hold up your hands, without speaking anymore."*

Our decision did not take long to reach.

We thought there was no reason to deliberate,

And granted him his way without further discussion,

And bade him tell us what he had decided, as he pleases.

790 *"Gentlemen," he said, "Now listen to my best advice;*

But I pray you, take it not in scorn.

This is the point, to speak short and plain,

That each of you, to shorten the long day,

Shall tell two stories as we journey

795 *Towards Canterbury, and I mean,*

On coming home, each shall tell another two,

All of adventures that have happened once upon a time.

And he who plays his part the best of all,

That is to say, who tells in this manner

800 *Tales of good morality , in most amusing mode,*

Shall have a supper at all the others' cost

Here in this room and sitting by this post,

When we come back again from Canterbury.

And for to make yow the moore mury,

805 I wol myselven goodly with yow ryde

Right at myn owene cost, and be youre gyde;

And who so wole my juggement withseye

Shal paye al that we spenden by the weye.

And if ye vouche sauf that it be so,

810 Tel me anon, withouten wordes mo,

And I wol erly shape me therfore."

This thyng was graunted, and oure othes swore

With ful glad herte, and preyden hym also

That he wolde vouche sauf for to do so,

815 And that he wolde been oure governour,

And of our tales juge and reportour,

And sette a soper at a certeyn pris,

And we wol reuled been at his devys

In heigh and lough; and thus by oon assent

820 We been acorded to his juggement.

And therupon the wyn was fet anon;

We dronken, and to reste wente echon,

Withouten any lenger taryynge.

Amorwe, whan that day bigan to sprynge,

825 Up roos oure Hoost, and was oure aller cok,

And gadrede us to gidre alle in a flok,

And forth we riden, a litel moore than paas

Unto the wateryng of Seint Thomas;

And there oure Hoost bigan his hors areste

830 And seyde, "Lordynges, herkneth if yow leste.

Ye woot youre foreward, and I it yow recorde.

If even-song and morwe-song accorde,

Lat se now who shal telle the firste tale.

53

And now, the more to warrant you'll be merry,

805 *I will myself, be glad to ride with you*

At my own expense, and I be your guide;

But whosoever shall not accept my judgment

Shall pay for everything we spend along the way.

And if you are agreed that it be so,

810 *Tell me immediately, without any further words,*

And I will then get ready early."

This thing was granted, and we swore our oaths,

With very joyful hearts, and prayed of him

That he would consent to do so,

815 *And that he would be our governor,*

Judging our tales, and be the score-keeper,

And arrange a supper at a certain price,

And we would be ruled by his desires

In things both great and small; and thus in unanimity

820 *We agreed to his judgment.*

And thereupon, the wine was fetched straightaway;

We drank, and then everyone went to rest,

Without any further delay.

Next morning, when the day began to dawn,

825 *Our Host rose, and acting as our rooster,*

He gathered us together in a flock,

And we rode forth at little more than a walking pace

Until the watering place of Saint Thomas;

And there our host pulled up his horse

830 *And said: "Gentlemen, listen if you please.*

You know what you promised, and I will recall it to you.

If [your assent at] even-song and morning-song is the same,

Let's now decide who shall tell the first tale.

As evere mote I drynke wyn or ale,

835 Whoso be rebel to my juggement

Shal paye for al that by the wey is spent.

Now draweth cut, er that we ferrer twynne,

He which that hath the shorteste shal bigynne.

Sire Knyght," quod he, "my mayster and my lord,

840 Now draweth cut, for that is myn accord.

Cometh neer," quod he, "my lady Prioresse,

And ye, Sir Clerk, lat be youre shamefastnesse,

Ne studieth noght; ley hond to, every man!"

Anon to drawen every wight bigan,

845 And shortly for to tellen as it was,

Were it by aventure, or sort, or cas,

The sothe is this, the cut fil to the Knyght,

Of which ful blithe and glad was every wyght.

And telle he moste his tale, as was resoun,

850 By foreward and by composicioun,-

As ye han herd, what nedeth wordes mo?

And whan this goode man saugh that it was so,

As he that wys was and obedient

To kepe his foreward by his free assent,

855 He seyde, "Syn I shal bigynne the game,

What, welcome be the cut, a Goddes name!

Now lat us ryde, and herkneth what I seye."

And with that word we ryden forth oure weye,

And he bigan with right a myrie cheere

860 His tale anon, and seyde as ye may heere.

Here endeth the prologe of this book

And as I hope to drink more wine and ale,

835 Whomsoever rebels against my judgment

Shall pay for all that is spent along the way.

Now draw straws, before we go any further,

And he that draws the shortest shall begin.

Sir Knight," said he, "my master and my lord,

840 You shall draw first as you have pledged your word.

Come near," said he, "my lady Prioress,

And you, sir Clerk, put your modesty aside,

No more study; every man lay hands on a straw!"

At once, everyone began to draw,

845 And, to make short the matter, as it was,

Whether by chance or whatsoever cause,

The truth is, that the Knight drew the shortest straw,

For which everyone was very happy and pleased.

And he must tell his tale, as was proper,

850 According to the promise and agreement,-

As you have heard, what need is there for more words?

And when this good man saw that it was so,

Being that he was wise and obedient

He kept his agreement given by free assent,

855 He said: "Since I shall begin the game,

What, welcome be the draw, and in God's name!

Now let us ride, and listen to what I say."

And with that word we rode forth on our way,

And he began with a very merry humour

860 To tell his tale straight away, as you may hear.

Here ends the Prologue of this book; ..

56

The Pardoner's Introduction, Prologue and Tale

The Introduction to the Pardoner's Tale

The Wordes of the Hoost to the Phisicien and the Pardoner

Oure Hooste gan to swere as he were wood;
"Harrow!" quod he, "by nayles and by blood!
This was a fals cherl and a fals justice!
As shameful deeth as herte may devyse

5   Come to thise juges and hire advocatz!
Algate this sely mayde is slayn, allas!
Allas, to deere boughte she beautee!
Wherfore I seye al day, as men may see
That yiftes of Fortune and of Nature

10   Been cause of deeth to many a creature.
(Hir beautee was hir deeth, I dar wel sayn;
Allas, so pitously as she was slayn!)
Of bothe yiftes that I speke of now
Men han ful ofte moore harm than prow.

15   But trewely, myn owene maister deere,
This is a pitous tale for to heere.
But nathelees, passe over is no fors;
I pray to God so save thy gentil cors,
And eek thyne urynals and thy jurdanes,

20   Thyn ypocras and eek thy galiones
And every boyste ful of thy letuarie,
God blesse hem, and oure lady Seinte Marie!
So moot I theen, thou art a propre man,
And lyk a prelat, by Seint Ronyan!

25   Seyde I nat wel? I kan nat speke in terme;
But wel I woot thou doost myn herte to erme,
That I almoost have caught a cardyacle.
By corpus bones, but I have triacle,
Or elles a draughte of moyste and corny ale,

The Introduction to the Pardoner's Tale

The Wordes of the Hoost to the Phisicien and the Pardoner

Our Host began to swear as if he were a lunatic;
"Alas!" Said he. "By the nails and blood of Christ!
This was a false peasant and a false justice!
As shameful a death as a heart can devise
5   *Come to these judges and their lawyers!*
Nevertheless, this poor maiden is slain, alas!
Her beauty was bought at too high a price!
Therefore I say all day, as we may see
That gifts of Fortune or Nature
10   *Are the cause of many a creature's death.*
(Her beauty was her death, I dare well say;
Alas, how pitifully she was slain!)
From both these gifts I spoke of now
Men often have more harm than profit.
15   *But truly, my own dear master,*
This tale is pitiful to hear.
But nonetheless pass it over; it does not matter;
I pray God to save thy gentle body,
And also your urine examining vessels and piss-pots,
20   *As well as your spiced sweet wines and your medicinal drinks*
And every box full of your liquid medicines,
God bless them and our Lady, the blessed Saint Mary!
As I live and prosper, you are a proper fellow,
And like a prelate, by Saint Ronan!
25   *Have I said this well? I do not know how to speak in technical terms;*
But I know well that you made my heart ache so,
Such that I have nearly had heart palpitations.
By Christ's bones unless I take medicine,
Or else a draught of fresh malty ale,

30	Or but I heere anon a myrie tale,
	Myn herte is lost, for pitee of this mayde!
	Thou beel amy, thou Pardoner," he sayde,
	"Telle us som myrthe or japes right anon."
	"It shal be doon," quod he, "by Seint Ronyon;
35	But first," quod he, "heere at this alestake,
	I wol bothe drynke and eten of a cake."
	But right anon the gentils gonne to crye,
	"Nay, lat hym telle us of no ribaudye!
	Telle us som moral thyng that we may leere
40	Som wit, and thanne wol we gladly heere!"
	"I graunte, ywis," quod he, "but I moot thynke
	Upon som honeste thyng, while that I drynke."

Heere folweth the Prologe of the Pardoners Tale

Radix malorum est Cupiditas. Ad Thimotheum

	"Lordynges," quod he, "in chirches whan I preche,
	I peyne me to han an hauteyn speche,
45	And rynge it out as round as gooth a belle,
	For I kan al by rote that I telle.
	My theme is alwey oon and evere was -
	'*Radix malorum est Cupiditas*.'
	First I pronounce whennes that I come,
50	And thanne my bulles shewe I, alle and some;
	Oure lige lordes seel on my patente,
	That shewe I first, my body to warente,
	That no man be so boold, ne preest ne clerk,
	Me to destourbe of Cristes hooly werk.
55	And after that thanne telle I forth my tales,
	Bulles of popes and of cardynales,
	Of patriarkes and bishopes I shewe,

30	*Or hear a merry tale straight away,*
	Mine heart is lost, in pity for this maid!
	"You good friend, you Pardoner," he said,
	"Tell us some mirth or comic tales right now."
	"It shall be done," he said, "By Saint Ronan;"
35	*"But first" he said, "here at this ale-house,*
	I will drink and eat a bit of bread."
	But immediately the gentle people began to call out,
	"No, do not let him tell us some ribald tale!
	Tell us some moral thing that we may learn
40	*Some wisdom, and then will we gladly listen!"*
	"I agree, certainly," he said, "but I must have time to think
	Upon some righteous thing while I drink."

Here follows the Prologue of the Pardoner's Tale.

Greed is the root of all evil, Epist Timothy Chpt 6,

	"Gentlemen," he said, "when I preach in churches,
	I strive for a resounding voice,
45	*And I ring it out as round as a bell,*
	For I know by heart all that I say.
	My theme is and always was one and the same -
	'Greed is the root of all evil.'
	"First I pronounce where I come from,
50	*And then I show my papal bulls, one and all;*
	[But] it is the seal of our liege lord the king on my credentials,
	That I show first to protect myself,
	Lest any man, priest, or clerk would be so bold,
	As to disturb me in Christ's holy labours.
55	*After that I then proceed with my tales,*
	Of bulls of popes and of cardinals,
	Of patriarchs and bishops I show,

And in Latyn I speke a wordes fewe,

To saffron with my predicacioun,

60 And for to stire hem to devocioun.

Thanne shewe I forth my longe cristal stones,

Ycrammed ful of cloutes and of bones;

Relikes been they, as wenen they echoon.

Thanne have I in latoun a sholder-boon

65 Which that was of an hooly Jewes sheepe.

'Goode men,' I seye, 'taak of my wordes keepe;

If that this boon be wasshe in any welle,

If cow, or calf, or sheep, or oxe swelle,

That any worm hath ete, or worm ystonge,

70 Taak water of that welle, and wassh his tonge,

And it is hool anon; and forthermoor,

Of pokkes and of scabbe and every soore

Shal every sheepe be hool that of this welle

Drynketh a draughte. Taak kepe eek what I telle,

75 If that the goode man that the beestes oweth,

Wol every wyke, er that the cok hym croweth,

Fastynge, drinken of this welle a draughte,

As thilke hooly Jew oure eldres taughte,

Hise beestes and his stoor shal multiplie.

80 And, sires, also it heeleth jalousie;

For though a man be falle in jalous rage,

Lat maken with this water his potage,

And nevere shal he moore his wyf mystriste,

Though he the soothe of hir defaute wiste,

85 Al had she taken preestes two or thre.

Heere is a miteyn eek, that ye may se.

He that his hand wol putte in this mitayn,

He shal have multipliyng of his grayn

What he hath sowen, be it whete or otes,

And I speak a few words in Latin,

To add spice to my preaching,

60 *And to stir men to devotion.*

Then I show forth my long glass cases,

Crammed full of cloths and bones;

Which everyone believes are holy relics.

I even have a shoulder-bone set in brass

65 *Which came from a holy Jew's sheep.*

'Good men,' I say, 'mark my words;

If this bone is washed in any spring,

And if a cow or calf or sheep or ox swell up,

That has been stung or bitten by any serpent,

70 *Take water from that spring and rinse its tongue,*

And it will heal immediately. And furthermore,

Of pox or scabs or every sore

Every sheep shall be cured by this spring

That drinks a draught [from it]. Mark what I say,

75 *If the man of the house who owns beasts,*

Would, every week before the cock crows,

Drink a draught from this spring whilst fasting,

As this holy Jew taught our forefathers,

His beasts and his stock shall thereby multiply.

80 *And sirs, it will cure jealousy also;*

For although a man fall into a jealous fury,

Mix his broth with this water,

And he will never mistrust his wife again,

Even if he knows the very truth of her fault,

85 *Although she has taken two or three priests.*

You may see that I also have a glove.

He who will put his hand in this glove,

He shall see the grain he has sown multiply

Whether it is wheat or barley,

90   So that he offre pens, or elles grotes.

Goode men and wommen, o thyng warne I yow,

If any wight be in this chirche now

That hath doon synne horrible, that he

Dar nat for shame of it yshryven be,

95   Or any womman, be she yong or old,

That hath ymaad hir housbonde cokewold,

Swich folk shal have no power ne no grace

To offren to my relikes in this place.

And who so fyndeth hym out of swich fame,

100   He wol come up and offre, on Goddes name,

And I assoille him, by the auctoritee

Which that by tulle ygraunted was to me."

By this gaude have I wonne, yeer by yeer,

An hundred mark, sith I was pardoner.

105   I stonde lyk a clerk in my pulpet,

And whan the lewed peple is doun yset,

I preche so, as ye han heerd bifoore,

And telle an hundred false japes moore.

Thanne peyne I me to strecche forth the nekke,

110   And est and west upon the peple I bekke,

As dooth a dowve sittynge on a berne.

Myne handes and my tonge goon so yerne

That it is joye to se my bisynesse.

Of avarice and of swich cursednesse

115   Is al my prechyng, for to make hem free

To yeven hir pens; and namely, unto me!

For myn entente is nat but for to wynne,

And no thyng for correccioun of synne.

rekke nevere, whan that they been beryed,

120   Though that hir soules goon a-blakeberyed!

For certes, many a predicacioun

65

90	So he will offer [me] pennies, or else groats.
	'But, good men and women, of one thing I warn you,
	If any person is now in this church
	Who has committed a horrible sin and
	Dares not to be confessed of it because of shame,
95	Or if any woman, be she old or young,
	Has been unfaithful to her husband,
	Such people shall have no power or grace
	To make offerings here to my relics.
	But whoever knows himself to be free from such fault,
100	Let him come up and make an offering in the name of God,
	And I will absolve him by the authority
	Which has been granted to me by papal bull."
	By this trickery I have gained every year,
	A hundred marks since becoming a pardoner.
105	I stand like a cleric in my pulpit,
	And when the ignorant people sit down,
	I preach as you have heard ,
	And tell a hundred more false stories.
	Then I take pains to stretch out my neck,
110	And bob my head east and west over the people,
	Like a dove perched upon a barn.
	My hands and tongue move so quickly
	That it is a joy to see me at my business.
	Of avarice and such accursed things
115	Is what my preaching is about, for to make them generous
	In giving their money, and especially to me!
	My aim is all for profit,
	And nothing for the correction of sin.
	I do not care, when they are dead,
120	Even if their souls have gone blackberrying!
	Surely, many a sermon

Comth ofte tyme of yvel entencioun.

Som for plesance of folk, and flaterye,

To been avaunced by ypocrisye,

125 And som for veyne glorie, and som for hate.

For whan I dar noon oother weyes debate,

Thanne wol I stynge hym with my tonge smerte

In prechyng, so that he shal nat asterte

To been defamed falsly, if that he

130 Hath trespased to my bretheren, or to me.

For though I telle noght his propre name,

Men shal wel knowe that it is the same

By signes, and by othere circumstances.

Thus quyte I folk that doon us displesances,

135 Thus spitte I out my venym, under hewe

Of hoolynesse, to semen hooly and trewe.

But shortly, myn entente I wol devyse;

I preche of no thyng but for coveityse.

Therfore my theme is yet, and evere was,

140 '*Radix malorum est Cupiditas.*'

Thus kan I preche agayn that same vice

Which that I use, and that is avarice.

But though myself be gilty in that synne,

Yet kan I maken oother folk to twynne

145 From avarice, and soore to repente;

But that is nat my principal entente.

I preche no thyng but for coveitise.

Of this mateere it oghte ynogh suffise.

Thanne telle I hem ensamples many oon

150 Of olde stories longe tyme agoon.

For lewed peple loven tales olde;

Swiche thynges kan they wel reporte and holde.

What, trowe ye, the whiles I may preche,

Often comes from an evil intention.

Some to please and flatter people,

To aim for advancement through hypocrisy,

125 *And some for vain glory and some for hate.*

For when I dare not debate in other ways,

Then I sting him with my sharp tongue

When I preach, so that he cannot claim

To have been falsely defamed, if he

130 *Has trespassed against me or my brethren.*

For though I do not mention his name,

Men shall know whom I mean

By hints and other circumstances.

Thus I repay people who do unpleasant things to us pardoners,

135 *Thus I spit out my venom under the guise*

Of holiness, seeming holy and faithful.

I say again, in a few words;

I preach for no motive but greed.

Therefore my theme is and always was,

140 *'Greed is the root of all evil.'*

Thus I know how to preach against that same vice

Which I practice, and that is avarice.

But although I am guilty of that sin,

I know how to make other people turn away

145 *From avarice and repent sorely;*

But that is not my main purpose.

I do not preach for anything but greed.

And regarding this matter, this ought to be sufficient.

Then I tell them many examples

150 *From old stories of long ago.*

For ignorant people love old tales;

Such things they know well [to]remember and repeat.

What! Do you think that while I can preach,

And wynne gold and silver for I teche,

155 That I wol lyve in poverte wilfully?

Nay, nay, I thoghte it nevere, trewely!

For I wol preche and begge in sondry landes,

I wol nat do no labour with myne handes,

Ne make baskettes, and lyve therby,

160 By cause I wol nat beggen ydelly.

I wol noon of the apostles countrefete;

I wol have moneie, wolle, chese, and whete,

Al were it yeven of the povereste page,

Or of the povereste wydwe in a village,

165 Al sholde hir children sterve for famyne.

Nay, I wol drynke licour of the vyne,

And have a joly wenche in every toun.

But herkneth, lordynges, in conclusioun:

Your likyng is, that I shal telle a tale.

170 Now have I dronke a draughte of corny ale,

By God, I hope I shal yow telle a thyng

That shal by resoun been at youre likyng.

For though myself be a ful vicious man,

A moral tale yet I you telle kan,

175 Which I am wont to preche, for to wynne.

Now hoold youre pees! My tale I wol bigynne."

Heere bigynneth the Pardoners Tale

In Flaundres whilom was a compaignye

Of yonge folk, that haunteden folye,

As riot, hasard, stywes, and tavernes,

180 Wher as with harpes, lutes, and gyternes

They daunce and pleyen at dees, bothe day and nyght,

And eten also and drynken over hir myght,

69

And gain gold and silver for my teaching,

155   *That I shall live in poverty willingly?*

Nay, nay, truly I never thought of it!

I will preach and beg everywhere I go,

I will not do labour with my hands,

Nor make baskets by which to make my living,

160   *Because I will not be an idle beggar.*

I will not imitate any of the apostles;

I will have money, wool, cheese, and wheat,

Whether given by the poorest lad,

Or the poorest widow in a village,

165   *Even though her children starve.*

No, I will drink good wine,

And have a merry wench in every town.

But listen, gentlemen, in conclusion:

Your will is that I tell a tale.

170   *Now that I have drunk a good draught of malty beer,*

By the Lord I hope I shall tell you a thing

That shall by reason be to your liking.

For although I am a very vicious man,

I know how to tell you a moral tale,

175   *Which I am used to preach to make profit.*

Now hold your peace, and I will begin my tale."

Here begins the Pardoner's Tale.

Once there dwelt in Flanders a company

Of young people who made a habit of folly,

Such as debauchery, gambling, brothels, and taverns,

180   *Where with harps, lutes and citterns*

They danced and played at dice day and night,

And ate and drank more than their capacity,

Thurgh which they doon the devel sacrifise

Withinne that develes temple in cursed wise,

185   By superfluytee abhomynable.

Hir othes been so grete and so dampnable

That it is grisly for to heere hem swere.

Oure blissed lordes body they totere -

Hem thoughte that Jewes rente hym noght ynough -

190   And ech of hem at otheres synne lough.

And right anon thanne comen tombesteres,

Fetys and smale, and yonge frutesteres,

Syngeres with harpes, baudes, wafereres,

Whiche been the verray develes officeres

195   To kyndle and blowe the fyr of lecherye,

That is annexed unto glotonye.

The hooly writ take I to my witnesse,

That luxurie is in wyn and dronkenesse.

Lo, how that dronken Looth, unkyndely

200   Lay by hise doghtres two, unwityngly;

So dronke he was, he nyste what he wroghte.

Herodes, whoso wel the stories soghte,

Whan he of wyn was repleet at his feeste,

Right at his owene table he yaf his heeste

205   To sleen the Baptist John, ful giltelees.

Senec seith a good word, doutelees;

He seith, he kan no difference fynde

Bitwix a man that is out of his mynde,

And a man which that is dronkelewe,

210   But that woodnesse fallen in a shrewe

Persevereth lenger than dooth dronkenesse.

O glotonye, ful of cursednesse!

O cause first of oure confusioun!

O original of oure dampnacioun

Through which they made sacrifice to the Devil

Within the Devil's temples in an accursed manner,

185 *By their abominable excess.*

Their oaths were so great and so damnable

That it was grisly to hear them swear.

They tore our blessed Lord's body to pieces -

They thought the Jews had not torn him enough -

190 *And each laughed at the others' sins.*

And then the dancing girls came on straightaway,

Graceful and slim with young girls selling fruit,

Singers with harps, pimps and confectioners,

Who are all the Devil's true officers

195 *To kindle and blow that fire of lust,*

Which is allied to gluttony.

I take Holy Scripture as my witness,

That lechery is in wine and drunkenness.

Lo, how drunken Lot, against nature

200 *Lay with his daughters, unwittingly;*

He was so drunk he did not know what he had done.

Herod, any one may look up the story,

When he was full of wine at his feast,

Gave the command at his own table

205 *To slay the John the Baptist, without any guilt.*

Seneca, doubtless, also says a good word;

He says he can find no difference

Between a man that is out of his mind,

And a man who is addicted to drink,

210 *Except that madness, when it attacks an evil person*

Endures longer than drunkenness.

O gluttony, full of cursedness!

O first cause of our ruin!

O origin of our damnation

215	Til Crist hadde boght us with his blood agayn!
	Lo, how deere, shortly for to sayn,
	Aboght was thilke cursed vileynye!
	Corrupt was al this world for glotonye!
	Adam oure fader, and his wyf also,
220	Fro Paradys to labour and to wo
	Were dryven for that vice, it is no drede.
	For whil that Adam fasted, as I rede,
	He was in Paradys, and whan that he
	Eet of the fruyt deffended on the tree,
225	Anon he was out cast to wo and peyne.
	O glotonye, on thee wel oghte us pleyne!
	O, wiste a man how manye maladyes
	Folwen of excesse and of goltonyes,
	He wolde been the moore mesurable
230	Of his diete, sittynge at his table.
	Allas, the shorte throte, the tendre mouth
	Maketh that est and west and north and south
	In erthe, in eir, in water, man to swynke
	To gete a glotoun deyntee mete and drynke!
235	Of this matiere, O Paul! wel kanstow trete:
	"Mete unto wombe and wombe eek unto mete
	Shal God destroyen bothe," as Paulus seith.
	Allas, a foul thyng is it, by my feith,
	To seye this word, and fouler is the dede
240	Whan man so drynketh of the white and rede
	That of his throte he maketh his pryvee
	Thurgh thilke cursed superfluitee.
	The Apostel wepying seith ful pitously,
	"Ther walken manye of whiche yow toold have I -
245	I seye it now wepyng with pitous voys,
	That they been enemys of Cristes croys,

215   Until Christ has redeemed us with His blood again!

Lo, how dearly, shortly to say,

Was this cursed villainy paid for!

This whole world was ruined by gluttony!

Our father Adam and his wife as well,

220   From Paradise to labour and woe

Were driven out for that vice, there is no doubt.

For I read that while Adam fasted,

He lived in Paradise, and when he

Ate of the forbidden fruit of the tree,

225   He was immediately cast out to woe and pain.

O gluttony, well may we accuse you!

If a man only knew how many maladies

Follow from gluttony and excess,

He would be more moderate

230   In his diet as he sits at his table.

Alas! The short throat, the delicate mouth

Makes men east, west, north, and south,

Man labours in earth, air, and water

To provide a glutton with fine meat and drink!

235   On this, O Paul, well can you explain:

"Meat unto the belly and belly also to the meat,

God shall destroy both," as Paul says.

Alas!, by my faith, it is foul thing,

To say this word, but fouler is the deed

240   When a man so drinks of white and red wine

That he makes a toilet of his throat

Through this accursed excess.

The apostle, weeping, says piteously,

"There walk many of whom I have told you -

245   And I say it now weeping and with a piteous voice,

That they are enemies of Christ's cross,

Of whiche the ende is deeth, wombe is hir god."

O wombe! O bely! O stynkyng cod!

Fulfilled of donge and of corrupcioun,

250 At either ende of thee foul is the soun;

How greet labour and cost is thee to fynde,

Thise cookes, how they stampe, and streyne, and grynde,

And turnen substaunce into accident,

To fulfillen al thy likerous talent!

255 Out of the harde bones knokke they

The mary, for they caste noght awey,

That may go thurgh the golet softe and swoote;

Of spicerie, of leef, and bark, and roote,

Shal been his sauce ymaked by delit,

260 To make hym yet a newer appetit.

But, certes, he that haunteth swiche delices

Is deed, whil that he lyveth in tho vices.

A lecherous thyng is wyn, and dronkenesse

Is ful of stryvyng and of wrecchednesse.

265 O dronke man, disfigured is thy face!

Sour is thy breeth, foul artow to embrace,

And thurgh thy dronke nose semeth the soun,

As though thow seydest ay, "Sampsoun! Sampsoun!"

And yet, God woot, Sampsoun drank nevere no wyn!

270 Thou fallest, as it were a styked swyn;

Thy tonge is lost, and al thyn honeste cure;

For dronkenesse is verray sepulture

Of mannes wit and his discrecioun,

In whom that drynke hath dominacioun.

275 He kan no conseil kepe, it is no drede.

Now kepe yow fro the white and fro the rede,

And namely, fro the white wyn of Lepe,

That is to selle in fysshstrete, or in Chepe.

To which the end is death; the belly is their god."

O Guts, O Belly! O stinking bag!

Full of dung and corruption,

250   *That sounds foul coming out of either end:*

How great is the labour and costs needed to feed you,

How these cooks pound and strain and grind,

And transform basic provisions into an event,

To satisfy all your greedy desires!

255   *Out of the hard bone they knock*

The marrow, and throw away nothing,

That may pass through the gullet softly and sweetly;

Spiced with the leaf, bark, and root,

Shall his sauce be made for delight,

260   *To give him a new appetite.*

But, certainly, he that makes a habit of eating such delights

Is dead, while he lives in those vices.

Wine is a lecherous thing, and drunkenness

Is full of wretchedness and quarrelling.

265   *O drunken man, your face is disfigured!*

Your breath is sour, you art foul to embrace,

And the sound through your drunken nose seems,

As if you always said, "Sampson, Sampson!"

And yet, God knows, Sampson never drank wine!

270   *You fall like a stuck pig;*

Your tongue is lost, and so is your sense of decency;

For drunkenness is the very tomb

Of man's wit and discretion,

In whom that drink has power.

275   *Undoubtedly, he does not know how to keep a secret.*

Now keep yourself away from the white and red wine,

And especially from the white wine of Lepe,

That is sold in Fish Street, or Cheapside.

This wyn of Spaigne crepeth subtilly

280 In othere wynes, growynge faste by,

Of which ther ryseth swich fumositee,

That whan a man hath dronken draughtes thre

And weneth that he be at hoom in Chepe,

He is in Spaigne, right at the toune of Lepe,

285 Nat at the Rochele, ne at Burdeux toun;

And thanne wol he seye "Sampsoun, Sampsoun!"

But herkneth, lordynges, o word I yow preye,

That alle the sovereyn actes, dar I seye,

Of victories in the Olde Testament,

290 Thurgh verray God that is omnipotent

Were doon in abstinence and in preyere.

Looketh the Bible, and ther ye may it leere.

Looke, Attilla, the grete conquerour,

Deyde in his sleepe, with shame and dishonour,

295 Bledynge ay at his nose in dronkenesse.

A capitayn sholde lyve in sobrenesse;

And over al this avyseth yow right wel,

What was comaunded unto Lamwel,

Nat Samuel, but Lamwel, seye I -

300 Redeth the Bible and fynde it expresly,

Of wyn yevyng to hem that han justise.

Namoore of this, for it may wel suffise.

And now that I have spoken of glotonye,

Now wol I yow deffenden hasardrye.

305 Hasard is verray mooder of lesynges,

And of dedeite and cursed forswerynges,

Blaspheme of Crist, manslaughtre and wast also

Of catel and of tyme, and forthermo

It is repreeve and contrarie of honour

310 For to ben holde a commune hasardour.

This Spanish wine subtly creeps

280   *Into other wines growing nearby,*

From which such fumes arise,

That when a man takes three draughts of it

He believes himself to be at home in Cheapside,

He is in Spain, right in the town of Lepe,

285   *Not at Rochelle nor at Bordeaux town;*

And then he will say, "Sampson, Sampson!"

But listen, gentlemen, to one word, I ask you,

I dare say that the great acts,

Of victories in the Old Testament,

290   *Through the true omnipotent God*

Were done by abstinence and prayer.

Look into the Bible and there you may see it.

Look at Attila, the great conqueror,

Who died in his sleep in shame and disgrace,

295   *Bleeding at his nose in a drunkenness.*

A great captain should live soberly;

And furthermore, consider very carefully,

What was commanded to Lemuel,

Not Samuel, I say, but Lemuel-

300   *Read the Bible and find it expressly written,*

About giving wine to those responsible for doing justice.

But no more now, for this may well suffice.

Now that I have spoken of gluttony,

I will forbid gambling to you.

305   *Dice-playing is the very mother of lies,*

And of deceit, and cursed perjuries,

Blasphemy of Christ, manslaughter, and also a waste

Of money and of time; and furthermore

It is a disgrace and against honour

310   *To be known as a common dice-player.*

And ever the hyer he is of estaat,

The moore is he holden desolaat;

If that a prynce useth hasardrye,

In all governaunce and policye

315 He is as by commune opinioun

Yholde the lasse in reputacioun.

Stilboun, that was a wys embassadour,

Was sent to Corynthe in ful greet honour,

Fro Lacidomye to maken hire alliaunce.

320 And whan he cam hym happede par chaunce,

That alle the gretteste that were of that lond

Pleyynge atte hasard he hem fond.

For which, as soone as it myghte be,

He stal hym hoom agayn to his contree,

325 And seyde, "Ther wol I nat lese my name,

Ne I wol nat take on me so greet defame.

Yow for to allie unto none hasardours.

Sendeth othere wise embassadours,

For by my trouthe me were levere dye

330 Than I yow sholde to hasardours allye.

For ye that been so glorious in honours

Shul nat allyen yow with hasardours

As by my wyl, ne as by my tretee."

This wise philosophre, thus seyde hee.

335 Looke eek that to the kyng Demetrius

The kyng of Parthes, as the book seith us,

Sente him a paire of dees of gold, in scorn,

For he hadde used hasard ther-biforn,

For which he heeld his glorie or his renoun

340 At no value or reputacioun.

Lordes may fynden oother maner pley

Honeste ynough, to dryve the day awey.

And the higher a man's estate is,

The more shame he is considered to have;

If a prince practices dice-playing,

In all government and political affairs

315 *He will, by common opinion*

Be regarded as having lower reputation.

Stilbon, the wise ambassador,

Was sent to Corinth in great honour,

From Sparta to forge their alliance.

320 *And when he came he happened by chance,*

That the greatest men of that land

He found playing at dice.

For this reason, as soon as he could,

He went back to his home and country,

325 *And said, "I will not lose my good name there,*

Nor will I take on me such a great shame.

As to ally you with any dice-players.

Send other wise ambassadors,

For by my word I would rather die

330 *Than to ally you with dice-players.*

For you who has been so glorious in honours

Shall not be allied with dice-players

Through my will, or treaty of my making."

Thus spoke this wise philosopher.

335 *Also consider that to King Demetrius*

As the book tells us, was, by the king of the Parthians,

Sent him a pair of golden dice in mockery,

Because he had played dice before,

For which reason he held King Demetrius' glory or renown

340 *To be of no value or respect.*

Lords may find other kinds of diversions

Which are virtuous enough to pass their days away.

Now wol I speke of othes false and grete

A word or two, as olde bookes trete.

345 Gret sweryng is a thyng abhominable,

And fals sweryng is yet moore reprevable.

The heighe God forbad sweryng at al,

Witnesse on Mathew; but in special

Of sweryng seith the hooly Jeremye,

350 "Thou shalt seye sooth thyne othes, and nat lye,

And swere in doom, and eek in rightwisnesse";

But ydel sweryng is a cursednesse.

Bihoold and se, that in the firste table

Of heighe Goddes heestes honurable

355 How that the seconde heeste of hym is this:

"Take nat my name in ydel or amys."

Lo, rather he forbedeth swich sweryng

Than homycide, or any cursed thyng;

I seye, that as by ordre thus it stondeth,

360 This knowen that hise heestes understondeth

How that the seconde heeste of God is that.

And forther-over I wol thee telle al plat,

That vengeance shal nat parten from his hous

That of hise othes is to outrageous.

365 "By Goddes precious herte," and "by his nayles,"

And "By the blood of Crist that is in Hayles,

Sevene is my chaunce and thyn is cynk and treye!"

"By Goddes armes, if thou falsly pleye,

This daggere shal thurghout thyn herte go!"

370 This fruyt cometh of the bicched bones two,

Forsweryng, ire, falsnesse, homycide!

Now, for the love of Crist, that for us dyde,

Lete youre othes bothe grete and smale.

But, sires, now wol I telle forth my tale.

Now I will speak about false and great oaths

In a word or two as the old books discuss.

345   *Great swearing is an abominable thing,*

And false swearing is even more reproachful.

The almighty God, forbade any swearing at all,

As Matthew witnesses, but especially

The holy Jeremiah says of swearing,

350   *"You shall say your oaths in truth, and not lie,*

And swear in judgment and also in righteousness";

But idle swearing is a wicked thing.

See that in the first tablet

Of almighty God's commandments

355   *The second of His commandments is this:*

"Take not my name in vain or amiss."

See, He forbids such swearing

Before He forbids murder or many other cursed things;

I say that this is the order the commandments stand,

360   *Anyone who knows His commandments understands*

Why it is God's second commandment.

And furthermore, I tell you flatly,

That vengeance will not depart from the house

Of one who is too outrageous in his oaths.

365   *"By God's precious heart," and "by His nails,"*

And "By the blood of Christ in Hales Abbey,

My throw of the dice is seven and yours is five and three!"

"By God's arms, if you play falsely,

This dagger shall go through your heart!"

370   *This is the fruit that comes from two cursed dice,*

Perjury, anger, dishonesty, murder!

Now for the love of Christ who died for us,

Forsake your oaths, great and small.

But, sirs, I will now tell my tale.

375 Thise riotoures thre, of whiche I telle,

Longe erst er prime rong of any belle,

Were set hem in a taverne for to drynke.

And as they sat, they herde a belle clynke

Biforn a cors, was caried to his grave.

380 That oon of hem gan callen to his knave,

"Go bet," quod he, "and axe redily

What cors is this, that passeth heer forby;

And looke, that thou reporte his name weel."

"Sire," quod this boy, "it nedeth never a deel;

385 It was me toold, er ye cam heer two houres.

He was, pardee, an old felawe of youres;

And sodeynly he was yslayn to-nyght,

Fordronke, as he sat on his bench upright.

Ther cam a privee theef men clepeth Deeth,

390 That in this contree al the peple sleeth,

And with his spere he smoot his herte atwo,

And wente his wey withouten wordes mo.

He hath a thousand slayn this pestilence.

And, maister, er ye come in his presence,

395 Me thynketh that it were necessarie

For to be war of swich an adversarie.

Beth redy for to meete hym everemoore;

Thus taughte me my dame, I sey namoore."

"By Seinte Marie!" seyde this taverner,

400 "The child seith sooth, for he hath slayn this yeer

Henne over a mile, withinne a greet village

Bothe man and womman, child, and hyne, and page.

I trowe his habitacioun be there.

To been avysed, greet wysdom it were,

405 Er that he dide a man a dishonour."

"Ye, Goddes armes!" quod this riotour,

375	These three rioters of whom I speak,
	Long before any the early morning ring of any bell,
	Were sitting in a tavern to drink.
	And as they sat, they heard a bell tinkle
	That was being carried before a corpse to his grave.
380	One of them called to his servant,
	"Go quickly," he said, "and ask immediately
	What corpse passed by here;
	And see that you report his name correctly."
	"Sir," said the boy, "there is no need;
385	It was told to me two hours before you came.
	He was, indeed, an old friend of yours;
	Who was slain suddenly in the night,
	As he sat upright on his bench very drunk.
	There came a stealthy thief that men call Death,
390	Who slays all the people in this country,
	And with his spear and he struck his heart in two,
	And then went his way without more words.
	He has killed a thousand during this plague.
	And master, before you come into his presence,
395	I think it that it would be necessary
	To be wary of such an adversary.
	Be ready to meet him at all times;
	My mother taught me this. I can say no more."
	"By Blessed Mary," said the tavern-keeper,
400	"The child speaks the truth, for he hath slain this year
	In a large village over a mile from here
	Both man and woman, child, labourer, and servant boy.
	I believe his habitation is there.
	It would be great wisdom to be forewarned,
405	Before he does him disgrace or harm."
	"Yes, by God's arms!" said this rioter,

"Is it swich peril with hym for to meete?

I shal hym seke, by wey and eek by strete,

I make avow to Goddes digne bones!

410 Herkneth, felawes, we thre been al ones;

Lat ech of us holde up his hand til oother,

And ech of us bicomen otheres brother,

And we wol sleen this false traytour Deeth.

He shal be slayn, which that so manye sleeth,

415 By Goddes dignitee, er it be nyght!"

Togidres han thise thre hir trouthes plight

To lyve and dyen, ech of hem for oother,

As though he were his owene ybore brother;

And up they stirte al dronken in this rage,

420 And forth they goon towardes that village,

Of which the taverner hadde spoke biforn.

And many a grisly ooth thanne han they sworn,

And Cristes blessed body they torente -

Deeth shal be deed, if that they may hym hente!

425 Whan they han goon nat fully half a mile,

Right as they wolde han troden over a stile,

An oold man and a povre with hem mette.

This olde man ful mekely hem grette,

And seyde thus, "Now, lordes, God yow see!"

430 The proudeste of thise riotoures three

Answerde agayn, "What, carl, with sory grace,

Why artow al forwrapped save thy face?

Why lyvestow so longe in so greet age?"

This olde man gan looke in his visage,

435 And seyde thus: "For I ne kan nat fynde

A man, though that I walked into Ynde,

Neither in citee nor in no village,

That wolde chaunge his youthe for myn age;

"Is it really such a peril to meet with him?
I will seek him in the highways and the byways,
I vow to God's worthy bones.
410   *Listen, friends, we three are at one in this;*
Let each of us hold up his hand to the others,
And each of us becomes the others' brother,
And will slay this false traitor Death.
He who slays so many shall be slain,
415   *By God's dignity, before it is night!"*
The three pledged their word together
Each to live and die for the others,
As if he were his own-born brother;
And up they stood in this drunken fury,
420   *And they go forth toward that village,*
Of which the tavern-keeper had spoken before.
And many a grisly oath they then swore,
And Christ's blessed body they tore to pieces -
Death shall be dead if they can catch him!
425   *When they had gone not even half a mile,*
Just as they would have climbed over a stile,
They met an old and poor man,
This old man greeted them meekly,
And said, "Now, gentlemen, may God keep you well!"
430   *The haughtiest of these three rioters*
Answered, "What, peasant, bad luck to you,
Why are you completely wrapped up except your face?
Why do you live for so long to such an old age?"
This old man began to peer into his face,
435   *And said, "Because I know I will not find*
A man, even if I walk to India,
Neither in a city or a village in city or in village,
Who would exchange his youth for my age;

86

And therfore mooth I han myn age stille,

440 As longe tyme as it is Goddes wille.

Ne Deeth, allas, ne wol nat han my lyf.

Thus walke I lyk a restelees kaityf,

And on the ground, which is my moodres gate,

I knokke with my staf bothe erly and late,

445 And seye, "Leeve mooder, leet me in!

Lo, how I vanysshe, flessh and blood and skyn!

Allas, whan shul my bones been at reste?

Mooder, with yow wolde I chaunge my cheste,

That in my chambre longe tyme hath be,

450 Ye, for an heyre-clowt to wrappe me."

But yet to me she wol nat do that grace,

For which ful pale and welked is my face.

But, sires, to yow it is no curteisye

To speken to an old man vileynye,

455 But he trespasse in word, or elles in dede.

In Hooly Writ ye may yourself wel rede,

'Agayns an oold man, hoor upon his heed,

Ye sholde arise;' wherfore I yeve yow reed,

Ne dooth unto an oold man noon harm now,

460 Namoore than that ye wolde men did to yow

In age, if that ye so longe abyde.

And God be with yow where ye go or ryde.

I moote go thider, as I have to go."

"Nay, olde cherl, by God, thou shalt nat so,"

465 Seyde this oother hasardour anon;

"Thou partest nat so lightly, by Seint John!

Thou spak right now of thilke traytour Deeth,

That in this contree alle oure freendes sleeth.

Have heer my trouthe, as thou art his espye,

470 Telle where he is, or thou shalt it abye,

And therefore I must keep my old age,

440   For as long as it is God's will.

Alas, Death will not have my life.

Thus I walk like a restless wretch,

And on the ground, which is my mother's path,

I knock with my staff both early and late,

445   And say, "Dear mother, let me in!

See how I waste away, flesh and blood and skin!

Alas, when shall my bones be at peace?

Mother, I would exchange my valuables with you,

Which has been in my chamber for a long time,

450   For a shroud in which to wrap myself."

But still she will not do me that favour,

For which my face is pale and withered.

But sirs, it is not a courteous thing

To speak so rudely to an old man,

455   Unless he should trespass in word or else in deed.

You may read for yourselves in Holy Scripture,

"When you meet an old man with white hair on his head,

You shall arise.' For this reason I give you advice,

Do no harm now to an old man,

460   No more than you would like it to be done to you

In your old age, if you live so long.

And now God be with you, wherever you may walk or ride.

I must go where I have to go."

"Nay, old peasant, by God, you shall not [do] so,"

465   Said this other dice-player straight away;

"By St. John, you shall not depart so swiftly!

You spoke just now of that traitor Death

Who slays all our friends in this country-side.

By my word, you are his spy,

470   Tell where he is, or, you shall pay for it,

By God and by the hooly sacrament!

For soothly thou art oon of his assent

To sleen us yonge folk, thou false theef?"

"Now, sires," quod he, "if that ye be so leef

475   To fynde Deeth, turne up this croked wey,

For in that grove I lafte hym, by my fey,

Under a tree, and there he wole abyde;

Noght for your boost he wole him no thyng hyde.

Se ye that ook? Right ther ye shal hym fynde.

480   God save yow that boghte agayn mankynde,

And yow amende!" Thus seyde this olde man;

And everich of thise riotoures ran

Til he cam to that tree, and ther they founde

Of floryns fyne of gold ycoyned rounde

485   Wel ny an eighte busshels, as hem thoughte.

No lenger thanne after Deeth they soughte,

But ech of hem so glad was of that sighte,

For that the floryns been so faire and brighte,

That doun they sette hem by this precious hoord.

490   The worste of hem, he spak the firste word.

"Bretheren," quod he, "taak kepe what I seye;

My wit is greet, though that I bourde and pleye.

This tresor hath Fortune unto us yeven,

In myrthe and joliftee oure lyf to lyven,

495   And lightly as it comth, so wol we spende.

Ey, Goddes precious dignitee! Who wende

To-day that we sholde han so fair a grace?

But myghte this gold be caried fro this place

Hoom to myn hous or elles unto youres -

500   For wel ye woot that al this gold is oures -

Thanne were we in heigh felicitee.

But trewely, by daye it may nat bee;

By God and the Holy Sacrament!

For truly you are in conspiracy with him

To slay us young people, you false thief?"

"Now sirs," he said, "if you are so keen

475 To find Death, turn up this crooked path,

For, by my faith, I left him in that grove,

Under a tree, and there he will wait,

And for all your boasting, he will not hide.

Do you see that oak? You shall find him right there.

480 May God, who redeemed mankind, save you,

And remedy you!" Thus said this old man;

And each of these rioters ran

Until he came to that tree, and there they found

Florins coined of fine round gold

485 Nearly eight bushels, as it seemed to them.

They then no longer sought after Death,

But each was so glad at the sight,

For the florins were so beautiful and bright,

That they sat themselves down by this precious hoard.

490 The worst of them spoke first.

"Brethren," he said, "take heed of what I say;

My mind is sharp, even though I often jest and play around,

Now Fortune has given us this treasure,

So that we may spend our lives in mirth and jollity,

495 And as easily as it comes, so too we will spend it.

Ah! God's precious dignity! Who would have imagined

That we should have such great fortune today?

But if this gold be can be carried from this place

Home to my house, or else to yours -

500 For you know well that all this gold is ours -

Then would will be in great happiness.

But truly it may not be done during the day;

Men wolde seyn that we were theves stronge,
And for oure owene tresor doon us honge.

505 This tresor moste ycaried be by nyghte
As wisely and as slyly as it myghte.
Wherfore I rede that cut among us alle
Be drawe, and lat se wher the cut wol falle,
And he that hath the cut, with herte blithe

510 Shal renne to the towne, and that ful swithe,
And brynge us breed and wyn, ful prively;
And two of us shul kepen subtilly
This tresor wel, and if he wol nat tarie,
Whan it is nyght, we wol this tresor carie,

515 By oon assent, where as us thynketh best."
That oon of hem the cut broghte in his fest,
And bad hym drawe, and looke where it wol falle;
And it fil on the yongeste of hem alle,
And forth toward the toun he wente anon.

520 And al so soone, as that he was agon,
That oon of hem spak thus unto that oother,
"Thou knowest wel thou art my sworen brother;
Thy profit wol I telle thee anon.
Thou woost wel, that oure felawe is agon,

525 And heere is gold, and that ful greet plentee,
That shal departed been among us thre.
But nathelees, if I kan shape it so
That it departed were among us two,
Hadde I nat doon a freendes torn to thee?"

530 That oother answerde, "I noot hou that may be;
He woot how that the gold is with us tweye;
What shal we doon? What shal we to hym seye?"
"Shal it be conseil?" seyde the firste shrewe,
"And I shal tellen, in a wordes fewe,

Men would call us outright thieves,

And hang us for our own treasure.

505   This treasure must be carried by night

As wisely and slyly as we can.

Therefore, I advise that we have straws among us all

To draw and see where the cut will fall,

For he with the shortest shall, with a happy heart

510   Run quickly to the town,

And secretly bring us wine and bread;

And two of us shall carefully guard

This treasure well, and if he does not delay,

We will carry away the treasure when it is night,

515   By our agreement to wherever we think is best."

One of them put the straws in his fist,

And told them to draw to see where [the cut] will fall;

And it fell to the youngest of them all,

And he immediately went forth toward the town.

520   And as soon as he was gone,

One of them said to the other,

"You well know you are my sworn brother;

And straightaway I will tell you something to your profit.

You know well that our fellow has gone,

525   And here is gold in great abundance,

That shall be divided among the three of us.

But nevertheless, if we know how to organise it so

That if it was divided between us two,

Will I not have done you a friendly turn?"

530   The other answered, "I do not know how that can be;

He knows the gold was left with us two;

What shall we do? What shall we say to him?"

"Shall it be a secret?" said the first rogue,

"I shall tell you in few words,

535   What we shal doon, and bryngen it wel aboute."

"I graunte," quod that oother, "out of doute,

That by my trouthe I shal thee nat biwreye."

"Now," quod the firste, "thou woost wel we be tweye,

And two of us shul strenger be than oon.

540   Looke whan that he is set, that right anoon

Arys, as though thou woldest with hym pleye,

And I shal ryve hym thurgh the sydes tweye,

Whil that thou strogelest with hym as in game,

And with thy daggere looke thou do the same;

545   And thanne shal al this gold departed be,

My deere freend, bitwixen me and thee.

Thanne may we bothe oure lustes all fulfille,

And pleye at dees right at oure owene wille."

And thus acorded been thise shrewes tweye

550   To sleen the thridde, as ye han herd me seye.

This yongeste, which that wente unto the toun,

Ful ofte in herte he rolleth up and doun

The beautee of thise floryns newe and brighte.

"O lorde," quod he, "if so were that I myghte

555   Have al this tresor to my-self allone,

Ther is no man that lyveth under the trone

Of God, that sholde lyve so murye as I."

And atte laste the feend, oure enemy,

Putte in his thought that he sholde poyson beye,

560   With which he myghte sleen hise felawes tweye;

For-why, the feend foond hym in swich lyvynge

That he hadde leve hem to sorwe brynge.

For this was outrely his fulle entente,

To sleen hem bothe, and nevere to repente.

565   And forth he gooth, no lenger wolde he tarie,

Into the toun unto a pothecarie

535 *What we shall do to bring it about successfully."*

 "I agree," said the other, "without doubt,

 That by my word I will not to betray you."

 "Now," said the first, "you know well we are two,

 And that two of us shall be stronger than one.

540 *See to it that as soon as he when he is set down*

 Arise as if you would play sport with him,

 And I will stab him through the two sides,

 While you struggle with him as if in game,

 And you will do the same with your dagger;

545 *And then shall all this gold be divided,*

 My dear friend, between you and me.

 Then we may both fulfil all our desires,

 And play at dice when we wish."

 And thus were these two rogues agreed

550 *To slay the third, as you have heard me say.*

 The youngest, who was going to the town,

 Turned over in his heart continuously

 The beauty of those bright new florins.

 "O Lord," he said, "if it were that I might

555 *Have all this treasure to myself alone,*

 No man living under the throne

 Of God should live as merrily as I!"

 And at last the Devil, our enemy,

 Put it into his mind that he should buy poison,

560 *With which he might slay his two friends;*

 For the Devil found him living in such a way

 That he had permission to bring him to sorrow.

 For it was entirely his purpose,

 To slay them both and never to repent.

565 *And he went forth without further delay,*

 Into the town to an apothecary

And preyde hym that he hym wolde selle

Som poysoun, that he myghte hise rattes quelle;

And eek ther was a polcat in his hawe,

570 That, as he seyde, hise capouns hadde yslawe;

And fayn he wolde wreke hym, if he myghte,

On vermyn that destroyed hym by nyghte.

The pothecarie answerde, "And thou shalt have

A thyng, that al so God my soule save,

575 In al this world ther is no creature

That eten or dronken hath of this confiture

Noght but the montance of a corn of whete,

That he ne shal his lif anon forlete;

Ye, sterve he shal, and that in lasse while

580 Than thou wolt goon a paas nat but a mile,

This poysoun is so strong and violent."

This cursed man hath in his hond yhent

This poysoun in a box, and sith he ran

Into the nexte strete unto a man,

585 And borwed of hym large botels thre;

And in the two his poyson poured he;

The thridde he kepte clene for his owene drynke.

For al the nyght he shoop hym for to swynke

In cariynge of the gold out of that place.

590 And whan this riotour, with sory grace,

Hadde filed with wyn his grete botels thre,

To hise felawes agayn repaireth he.

What nedeth it to sermone of it moore?

For right as they hadde cast his deeth bifoore,

595 Right so they han him slayn, and that anon.

And whan that this was doon, thus spak that oon:

"Now lat us sitte and drynke, and make us merie,

And afterward we wol his body berie."

And asked that he would to sell him

Some poison so that he might kill his rats;

And also there was a pole-cat in his yard,

570   Which, he said, had killed his capons;

And he would gladly take revenge if he could,

On the pests which ruined him at night.

The apothecary answered "And you shall have

A thing, may God save my soul,

575   That no creature in all this world

Who eats or drinks this concoction

Even so little as that of a grain of wheat,

That shall not lose his life immediately;

Yes, he shall die, and will do so in less time

580   Than you can walk a mile,

This poison is so strong and violent."

This cursed man had taken in his hand

This box of poison, and then he ran

Into the next street to a man,

585   From whom he borrowed three large bottles;

And into two of them he poured his poison;

The third he kept clean for his own drink.

For he planned to work all night

Carrying away the gold from that place.

590   And when this rioter, with bad luck to him,

Had filled his three large bottles with wine,

He returned again to his friends.

What need is there to describe it more?

For just as they had planned his death before,

595   They killed him straight away.

And when this was done, one of them said:

"Now let us sit and drink and make us merry,

And afterwards we will bury his body."

And with that word it happed hym, par cas,

600 To take the botel ther the poysoun was,

And drank, and yaf his felawe drynke also,

For which anon they storven bothe two.

But certes, I suppose that Avycen

Wroot nevere in no canoun, ne in no fen,

605 Mo wonder signes of empoisonyng

Than hadde thise wrecches two, er hir endyng.

Thus ended been thise homycides two,

And eek the false empoysoner also.

O cursed synne ful of cursednesse!

610 O traytours homycide, O wikkednesse!

O glotonye, luxurie, and hasardrye!

Thou blasphemour of Crist, with vileynye

And othes grete, of usage and of pride,

Allas, mankynde, how may it bitide

615 That to thy Creatour which that the wroghte,

And with His precious herte-blood thee boghte,

Thou art so fals and so unkynde, allas!

Now, goode men, God foryeve yow youre trespas,

And ware yow fro the synne of avarice;

620 Myn hooly pardoun may yow alle warice,

So that ye offre nobles or sterlynges,

Or elles silver broches, spoones, rynges;

Boweth youre heed under this hooly bulle!

Com up, ye wyves, offreth of youre wolle!

625 Youre names I entre heer in my rolle anon,

Into the blisse of hevene shul ye gon.

I yow assoille by myn heigh power,

Yow that wol offre, as clene and eek as cleer

As ye were born. - And lo, sires, thus I preche.

630 And Jesu Crist, that is oure soules leche,

And with that word he happened, by chance,

600 *To take one bottle where the poison was,*

And he drank it, and gave his friend the drink as well,

For which they both quickly died.

But certainly, I suppose, that Avicenna

Never wrote in any canon nor chapter,

605 *A more wondrous description of the poisoning*

Than these two wretches had before they died.

Thus, these two murderers met their end,

As well as the false poisoner.

"O cursed sin full of cursedness!

610 *O treacherous homicide! O wickedness!*

O gluttony, lust and dice-playing!

You blasphemer of Christ with your evil

And great oaths, both habitual and with pride,

Alas mankind, how may it be

615 *That to your creator who made you,*

And who redeemed you with his precious heart's blood,

You are so false and deceitful, alas!

Now, good men, God forgives you your trespasses,

And be mindful that from the sin of avarice;

620 *My holy pardon will cure you all,*

If you offer me gold and silver coins,

Or else silver brooches, spoons, rings;

Bow your heads, bow them under this holy papal bull!

Come up, wives, offer up your wool!

625 *I will immediately enter your names here in my roll,*

And into heaven's bliss you shall go.

I absolve you by my high power,

So those who make such offerings, will become as clean and sinless

As when you were born. And lo, sirs, thus I preach.

630 *And may Jesus Christ, who is doctor to our souls,*

So graunte yow his pardoun to receyve,

For that is best, I wol yow nat deceyve.

But sires, o word forgat I in my tale:

I have relikes and pardoun in my male,

635   As faire as any man in Engelond,

Whiche were me yeven by the popes hond.

If any of yow wole of devocioun

Offren, and han myn absolucioun,

Com forth anon, and kneleth heere adoun,

640   And mekely receyveth my pardoun;

Or elles taketh pardoun as ye wende,

Al newe and fressh at every miles ende,

So that ye offren alwey, newe and newe,

Nobles or pens, whiche that be goode and trewe.

645   It is an honour to everich that is heer

That ye mowe have a suffisant pardoneer

T'assoille yow in contree as ye ryde,

For aventures whiche that may bityde.

Paraventure ther may fallen oon or two

650   Doun of his hors, and breke his nekke atwo.

Look, which a seuretee is it to yow alle

That I am in youre felaweship yfalle,

That may assoille yow, bothe moore and lasse,

Whan that the soule shal fro the body passe.

655   I rede that oure Hoost heere shal bigynne,

For he is moost envoluped in synne.

Com forth, sire Hoost, and offre first anon,

And thou shalt kisse my relikes everychon,

Ye, for a grote! unbokele anon thy purs.'

660   "Nay, nay," quod he, "thanne have I Cristes curs!

Lat be," quod he, "it shal nat be, so theech,

Thou woldest make me kisse thyn olde breech,

So grant that you may receive His pardon,

For that is better than mine, I will not deceive you.

"But sirs, one word I have forgotten in my tale:

Here in my bag I have relics and indulgences,

635   As fine as any man has in England,

Which were given to me by the pope's own hand.

If any of you would of devotion

Make an offering and have my absolution,

Come forth and kneel down here straightaway,

640   And meekly receive my pardon;

Or else take pardons as you travel,

And be all new and fresh, at the end of every mile,

Provided that you always offer, again and again,

Gold coins and silver pennies which are good and sound.

645   It is an honor to everyone here

That you have a pardoner with enough power

To absolve you as you ride through the countryside,

In case an accident might happen.

Perhaps one or two may fall

650   Down from their horses and break his neck in two.

Look what a security it is to you all

That I fell into your company,

And who can absolve you, both more and less,

When the soul shall pass from the body.

655   I advise that our Host here shall begin,

For he is most enveloped in sin.

Come forth, Sir Host, and offer straight away,

And you shall kiss all the relics,

Yes, for a groat; unbuckle your purse without delay."

660   No, no!" he said, "I will then have the curse of Christ!"

"Let me be;" he said, "it shall not be, I swear,

You would make me kiss your old pants,

And swere it were a relyk of a seint,

Though it were with thy fundement depeint.

665   But by the croys which that Seint Eleyne fond,

I wolde I hadde thy coillons in myn hond

In stide of relikes or of seintuarie.

Lat kutte hem of, I wol thee helpe hem carie;

They shul be shryned in an hogges toord."

670   This Pardoner answerde nat a word;

So wrooth he was, no word ne wolde he seye.

"Now," quod oure Hoost, "I wol no lenger pleye

With thee, ne with noon oother angry man."

But right anon the worthy Knyght bigan,

675   Whan that he saugh that al the peple lough,

"Namoore of this, for it is right ynough.

Sir Pardoner, be glad and myrie of cheere;

And ye, sir Hoost, that been to me so deere,

I prey yow, that ye kisse the pardoner;

680   And Pardoner, I prey thee, drawe thee neer,

And, as we diden lat us laughe and pley."

Anon they kiste, and ryden forth hir weye.

Heere is ended the Pardoners Tale.

And swear it is a saint's relic,

Even though it was stained by your own fundament.

665 But by the Holy Cross that St. Helen found,

I wish I had your testicles in my hand

Instead of relics or a receptacle for relics.

Let them be cut off, and I will help you carry them;

They shall be enshrined in a hog's turd."

670 This Pardoner answered not a word;

He was so angry, no word would he speak.

"Now," said our Host, "I will not play any longer

With you, nor with any other angry man."

But immediately the worthy Knight began,

675 When he saw all the people laugh,

"No more of this. For that is enough.

Sir Pardoner, be glad and cheerful;

And you, Sir Host, who is so dear to me,

I pray that you kiss the Pardoner;

680 And Pardoner, I pray you to draw near,

And let us laugh and play as we did before."

And without delay they kissed and rode on their way.

Here ends the Pardoner's Tale.

The Wife of Bath's Prologue and Tale

The Prologe of the Wyves Tale of Bathe

Experience, though noon auctoritee
Were in this world, were right ynogh to me
To speke of wo that is in mariage;
For, lordynges, sith I twelf yeer was of age,

5   Thonked be God, that is eterne on lyve,
Housbondes at chirche dore I have had fyve -
For I so ofte have ywedded bee -
And alle were worthy men in hir degree.
But me was toold, certeyn, nat longe agoon is,

10   That sith that Crist ne wente nevere but onis
To weddyng in the Cane of Galilee,
That by the same ensample, taughte he me,
That I ne sholde wedded be but ones.
Herkne eek, lo, which a sharpe word for the nones,

15   Biside a welle Jhesus, God and Man,
Spak in repreeve of the Samaritan.
"Thou hast yhad fyve housbondes," quod he,
"And thilke man the which that hath now thee
Is noght thyn housbonde;" thus seyde he certeyn.

20   What that he mente ther by, I kan nat seyn;
But that I axe, why that the fifthe man
Was noon housbonde to the Samaritan?
How manye myghte she have in mariage?
Yet herde I nevere tellen in myn age

25   Upon this nombre diffinicioun.
Men may devyne, and glosen up and doun,
But wel I woot, expres, withoute lye,
God bad us for to wexe and multiplye;
That gentil text kan I wel understonde.

30   Eek wel I woot, he seyde, myn housbonde

The Prologue of the Wife of Bath's Tale

Experience, rather than written authority,

Conflicts in this world, which makes it good enough for me,

To speak of the woe that is married life;

For, Gentlemen, since I was twelve years of age,

5   Thanks be to God, who lives in eternity,

I have had five husbands at the church door;

For I have been married that often ;

And all were worthy men in their rank.

But someone told me not long ago

10   That since Our Lord went only once

To a wedding in the Cana of Galilee,

That by the same example, He taught me,

I should have married no more than once.

Listen to what sharp words, were said on the occasion,

15   Beside a well by Jesus, God and man,

Spoke in reproach of the Samaritan:

'For thou hast had five husbands,' He said,

'And the man who has you now

Is not thine husband.' Thus He said with certainty,

20   What He meant by that, I do not know;

But I would ask now why that same fifth man

Was not husband to the Samaritan?

How many men could she have in marriage?

For I have never heard, in all my years,

25   A clear definition of this number,

[Although] men may guess and argue continuously.

But I know very well and can say, without lying,

God commanded us to be fruitful and multiply;

That noble text I know [and] well understand.

30   Also I know well, He said, that my husband

Sholde lete fader and mooder, and take to me;

But of no nombre mencioun made he,

Of bigamye, or of octogamye;

Why sholde men speke of it vileynye?

35   Lo, heere the wise kyng, daun Salomon;

I trowe he hadde wyves mo than oon-

As, wolde God, it leveful were to me

To be refresshed half so ofte as he!

Which yifte of God hadde he, for alle hise wyvys!

40   No man hath swich that in this world alyve is.

God woot, this noble kyng, as to my wit,

The firste nyght had many a myrie fit

With ech of hem, so wel was hym on lyve!

Yblessed be God, that I have wedded fyve;

45   (Of whiche I have pyked out the beste,

Bothe of here nether purs and of here cheste.

Diverse scoles maken parfyt clerkes,

And diverse practyk in many sondry werkes

Maketh the werkman parfyt sekirly;

50   Of fyve husbondes scoleiyng am I.)

Welcome the sixte, whan that evere he shal.

For sothe I wol nat kepe me chaast in al.

Whan myn housbonde is fro the world ygon,

Som Cristen man shal wedde me anon.

55   For thanne th'apostle seith that I am free,

To wedde, a Goddes half, where it liketh me.

He seith, that to be wedded is no synne,

Bet is to be wedded than to brynne.

What rekketh me, thogh folk seye vileynye

60   Of shrewed Lameth and of bigamye?

I woot wel Abraham was an hooly man,

And Jacob eek, as ferforth as I kan,

Should leave his father and mother, and take with me;

But He mentioned no specific number,

Whether of bigamy or of octogamy;

Why should men speak of it with contempt?

35   *Lo, listen to the wise old king, lord Solomon;*

I understand he had more than one wife;

Would that God made it permissible for me

To be comforted [just] half as often as he!

What a gift from God he had for all those wives!

40   *No living man in this world has such as that.*

God knows, this noble king, it strikes my mind,

The first night he had many a merry adventure

With each of them, so fortunate he was in life!

Praise be to God, that I have wedded five!

45   *(Of whom I picked out the best*

Both for their testicles and for their valuables

Different schools make perfect scholars,

And learning different methods in various works

Certainly makes the good workman perfect;

50   *For I have been schooled by five husbands.)*

A sixth husband is welcomed, whenever he shall arrive.

For truth, I will not keep myself chaste for ever;

When my husband is gone from this world,

Some Christian man shall marry me straight away;

55   *For then, St Paul says that I am free*

To wed, in God's name, where it pleases me.

He says that to be wedded is no sin;

Better to marry than to burn.

What care do I have, if folk speak evil

60   *Of accursed Lamech and his bigamy?*

I know well Abraham was holy man,

And Jacob also, as far as I know;

And ech of hem hadde wyves mo than two,

And many another holy man also.

65 Whanne saugh ye evere in any manere age,

That hye God defended mariage

By expres word? I pray you, telleth me,

Or where comanded he virginitee?

I woot as wel as ye it is no drede,

70 Th'apostel, whan he speketh of maydenhede;

He seyde that precept therof hadde he noon.

Men may conseille a womman to been oon,

But conseillyng is no comandement;

He putte it in oure owene juggement.

75 For hadde God comanded maydenhede,

Thanne hadde he dampned weddyng with the dede;

And certein, if ther were no seed ysowe,

Virginitee, wherof thanne sholde it growe?

Poul dorste nat comanden, atte leeste,

80 A thyng of which his maister yaf noon heeste.

The dart is set up of virginitee;

Cacche who so may, who renneth best lat see.

But this word is nat taken of every wight,

But ther as God lust gyve it of his myght.

85 I woot wel, th'apostel was a mayde;

But nathelees, thogh that he wroot and sayde

He wolde that every wight were swich as he,

Al nys but conseil to virginitee;

And for to been a wyf, he yaf me leve

90 Of indulgence, so it is no repreve

To wedde me, if that my make dye,

Withouten excepcioun of bigamye.

Al were it good no womman for to touche,

He mente, as in his bed or in his couche;

And each of them had more than two wives;

And many other holy men as well.

65   *When can you say, in any past era,*

That almighty God forbade marriage

By [His] express word? I pray you, tell me.

Or where He commanded virginity?

There is no doubt that I know as well as you,

70   *That when St Paul speaks about maidenhood;*

He said, he had no such commandment from the Lord.

Men may advise a woman to be one [a virgin],

But advice is not a commandment;

He left the matter to our own judgment.

75   *For had Lord God commanded maidenhood,*

He would then have damned marriage by the same deed;

And certainly, if there were no [new] seeds sown,

Where then would virgins be grown?

St Paul dared not to command us, at the least,

80   *A thing which his Master had not commanded.*

Virginity is set up to be the prize;

Catch it whosoever can; let us see who chases the best.

But this request is not meant for every person,

But [only] where God, in his power, desires it.

85   *I know well that St Paul was a virgin;*

But, nevertheless, although he wrote and said

He wished that every person were such as he,

Although that is nothing but advice to be a virgin;

And so to be a wife, he gave me leave

90   *By His indulgence, so there is no disgrace*

To marry me, if my mate should die,

Without being accused of bigamy.

Although it is best that a woman is not touched [by a man],

He meant, in his own bed or on his couch;

95   For peril is bothe fyr and tow t'assemble;

Ye knowe what this ensample may resemble.

This is al and som, he heeld virginitee

Moore parfit than weddyng in freletee.

Freletee clepe I, but if that he and she

100   Wolde leden al hir lyf in chastitee.

I graunte it wel, I have noon envie,

Thogh maydenhede preferre bigamye;

Hem liketh to be clene, body and goost.

Of myn estaat I nyl nat make no boost,

105   For wel ye knowe, a lord in his houshold,

He nath nat every vessel al of gold;

Somme been of tree, and doon hir lord servyse.

God clepeth folk to hym in sondry wyse,

And everich hath of God a propre yifte -

110   Som this, som that, as hym liketh shifte.

Virginitee is greet perfeccioun,

And continence eek with devocioun.

But Crist, that of perfeccioun is welle,

Bad nat every wight he sholde go selle

115   Al that he hadde, and gyve it to the poore,

And in swich wise folwe hym and his foore.

He spak to hem that wolde lyve parfitly,

And lordynges, by youre leve, that am nat I.

I wol bistowe the flour of myn age

120   In the actes and in fruyt of mariage.

Telle me also, to what conclusion

Were membres maad of generacion,

And of so parfit wys a wright ywroght?

Trusteth right wel, they were maad for noght.

125   Glose whoso wole, and seye bothe up and doun,

That they were maked for purgacioun

95   *For there is danger when mixing both fire and tinder;*

You know what this example means.

This is the sum total: he held that virginity

Is more perfect than marrying in moral weakness.

I call it moral weakness unless he and she

100   *Would live their whole lives in chastity.*

I fully accept this, [but] I do not envy it.

Though maidenhood is preferred to bigamy;

Let those who desire being clean of body and soul,

I will not make any boast about my situation.

105   *For well you know, a lord in his household,*

He does not have every vessel [made] all of gold;

Some made of wood, are [still] used in the lord's service.

God calls folk unto Him in sundry ways,

And everyone has an appropriate gift from God -

110   *Some this, some that, as it pleases Him to bestow.*

Virginity is a great perfection,

And also devout abstinence.

But Christ, who is the source of perfection,

Did not bid every person that he should go sell

115   *All that he had and give it to the poor,*

And in such manner follow Him in his foot steps.

He spoke to those that wanted to live perfectly;

And gentlemen, by your leave, that is not me.

I will devote the best years of my life

120   *To the acts and fruits of marriage.*

Tell me also, for what [other] purpose

Were genitals made for reproduction,

By such a perfect and wise craftsman?

Believe me, they were not made for nothing.

125   *Whoever interprets that way must argue continuously,*

That they were made for the passing out

Of uryne, and oure bothe thynges smale
Were eek to knowe a femele from a male,
And for noon other cause, -say ye no?
130 The experience woot wel it is noght so.
So that the clerkes be nat with me wrothe,
I sey this: that they maked ben for bothe,
That is to seye, for office and for ese
Of engendrure, ther we nat God displese.
135 Why sholde men elles in hir bookes sette
That man shal yelde to his wyf hire dette?
Now wherwith sholde he make his paiement,
If he ne used his sely instrument?
Thanne were they maad upon a creature
140 To purge uryne, and eek for engendrure.
But I seye noght that every wight is holde,
That hath swich harneys as I to yow tolde,
To goon and usen hem in engendrure.
Thanne sholde men take of chastitee no cure.
145 Crist was a mayde, and shapen as a man,
And many a seint, sith that the world bigan;
Yet lyved that evere in parfit chastitee.
I nyl envye no virginitee.
Lat hem be breed of pured whete-seed,
150 And lat us wyves hoten barly-breed;
And yet with barly-breed, Mark telle kan,
Oure Lord Jhesu refresshed many a man.
In swich estaat as God hath cleped us
I wol persevere; I nam nat precius.
155 In wyfhod I wol use myn instrument
As frely as my Makere hath it sent.
If I be daungerous, God yeve me sorwe!
Myn housbonde shal it have bothe eve and morwe,

Of urine, and that both of our little things

Were also to tell a female from a male,

And for no other purpose - say you not?

130 *Experience knows very well that it is not so.*

And, so the scholars will not be angry with me,

I say that they have been made for both [purposes],

That is to say, for function and for the benefit

Of reproduction, when we do not offend God.

135 *Why else should men set in their account book*

That man shall pay unto his wife her debt?

Now, with what should he make his payment,

If he did not use his blessed tool?

Then were these things were fashioned on the body

140 *For urination and also for procreation.*

But I do not say that every person is bound,

Who has such tackle, about which I told you,

To go and use it for procreation;

Then men would have no care about chastity.

145 *Christ was a virgin, and shaped like a man,*

And many a saint, since this world began,

Has lived in perfect chastity.

I do not resent their virginity;

Let them be bread of purest [white] wheat-seed,

150 *And let us wives be called barley bread;*

And yet with barley bread, [as] Mark tells us he knows,

Jesus Our Lord nourished many a man.

Into such status as God has called us

I will persevere, I am not fastidious.

155 *In wifehood I will use my womanly parts*

As freely as my Maker sent it to me

If I am reluctant [to provide sex], God will give me sorrow!

My husband shall have it both evening and morning,

Whan that hym list come forth and paye his dette.

160 An housbonde I wol have, I wol nat lette,

Which shal be bothe my dettour and my thral,

And have his tribulacioun withal

Upon his flessh whil that I am his wyf.

I have the power durynge al my lyf

165 Upon his propre body, and noght he.

Right thus the Apostel tolde it unto me,

And bad oure housbondes for to love us weel.

Al this sentence me liketh every deel" -

Up stirte the Pardoner, and that anon;

170 "Now, dame," quod he, "by God and by Seint John!

Ye been a noble prechour in this cas.

I was aboute to wedde a wyf; allas!

What sholde I bye it on my flessh so deere?

Yet hadde I levere wedde no wyf to-yeere!"

175 "Abyde," quod she, "my tale in nat bigonne.

Nay, thou shalt drynken of another tonne,

Er that I go, shal savoure wors than ale.

And whan that I have toold thee forth my tale

Of tribulacioun in mariage,

180 Of which I am expert in al myn age,

This to seyn, myself have been the whippe, -

Than maystow chese wheither thou wolt sippe

Of thilke tonne that I shal abroche,

Be war of it, er thou to ny approche;

185 For I shal telle ensamples mo than ten.

Whoso that nyl be war by othere men,

By hym shul othere men corrected be.

The same wordes writeth Ptholomee;

Rede it in his Almageste, and take it there."

190 "Dame, I wolde praye yow, if youre wyl it were,"

Whenever he desires to come forth and pay his debt.

160 *I will not stop, I will get a husband*

Who shall be both my debtor and my slave

And, in addition, shall have his troubles [placed]

Upon his body, for so long as I am his wife.

I have the power during all my life

165 *Over his own body, not he.*

For thus, St Paul told it unto me;

And commanded our husbands to love us dearly.

Every part of this lesson pleases me."

Immediately the Pardoner jumped up.

170 *"Now lady," he said, "by God and by Saint John,*

You have been a noble preacher in this matter!

Alas, I was about to wed a wife!

[But] why should I pay such a high price with my body?

I would rather not wed a wife this year."

175 *"But wait," she said, "my tale is not [yet] begun;*

No, you shall drink from another barrel

Before I go, and which shall taste worse than ale.

And when I have told you my tale

Of the troubles in marriage,

180 *About which, given my age, I am now an expert,*

This to say, I have myself been the whip,

Then may you choose whether you will sip

Out of that very barrel which I shall tap.

[But] beware of it, before you approach too near;

185 *For I shall give more than ten examples.*

Whosoever is not warned by the experience of others,

Shall become an example by which other men are corrected.

The same words were written by Ptolemy;

Read it in his Almagest and find it there."

190 *Madam, I pray you, if you were to so will it,"*

Seyde this Pardoner, "as ye bigan,

Telle forth youre tale, spareth for no man,

And teche us yonge men of your praktike."

"Gladly," quod she, "sith it may yow like.

195   But yet I praye to al this compaignye,

If that I speke after my fantasye,

As taketh not agrief of that I seye,

For myn entente nis but for to pleye."

Now, sire, now wol I telle forth my tale,

200   As evere moote I drynken wyn or ale,

I shal seye sooth, tho housbondes that I hadde,

As thre of hem were goode, and two were badde.

The thre men were goode, and riche, and olde;

Unnethe myghte they the statut holde

205   In which that they were bounden unto me-

Ye woot wel what I meene of this, pardee!

As help me God, I laughe whan I thynke

How pitously a-nyght I made hem swynke.

And, by my fey, I tolde of it no stoor,

210   They had me yeven hir gold and hir tresoor;

Me neded nat do lenger diligence

To wynne hir love, or doon hem reverence,

They loved me so wel, by God above,

That I ne tolde no deyntee of hir love.

215   A wys womman wol sette hire evere in oon

To gete hire love, ther as she hath noon.

But sith I hadde hem hoolly in myn hond,

And sith they hadde me yeven all hir lond,

What sholde I taken heede hem for to plese,

220   But it were for my profit and myn ese?

I sette hem so a-werke, by my fey,

That many a nyght they songen "weilawey!"

Said the Pardoner, "as you began,

Tell forth your tale, spare nothing for any man,

And teach us younger men about your technique."

"Gladly," she said, "since it may please you.

195   *But yet I request to all this company,*

That if I speak from my own fantasy,

They will not take offence about the things I say;

For my intention is for nothing but to play.

Now, gentlemen, I will now tell you my tale.

200   *And as I may drink wine or ale continuously,*

I shall tell the truth about the husbands that I've had,

For three of them were good, and two were bad.

The three good men were rich and [so] old.

They could barely perform the contractual obligation

205   *By which they were bound to me.*

By God, you know very well what I mean by that!

So help me God, I laugh now when I think

How pitifully I made them work at night;

And, by my faith, I set no store by it.

210   *They had [already] given me their gold, and their treasure;*

[So] I no longer needed to be diligent

To win their love, or show them respect.

By God above, they loved me so much,

[But] I never set [any] value on their love.

215   *A wise woman will strive continuously*

To obtain love for herself, when she has none.

But since I had them wholly in my hand,

And since they had given me all their land,

Why should I take any heed and try to please them,

220   *Unless it was for my own profit and pleasure?*

So, by my faith, I set them so to work,

That many a night they cried out 'Alas!'

The bacon was nat fet for hem, I trowe,

That som men han in Essex at Dunmowe.

225   I governed hem so wel after my lawe,

That ech of hem ful blisful was, and fawe

To brynge me gaye thynges fro the fayre.

They were ful glad whan I spak to hem faire,

For, God it woot, I chidde hem spitously.

230   Now herkneth hou I baar me proprely,

Ye wise wyves, that kan understonde.

Thus shul ye speke and bere hem wrong on honde;

For half so boldely kan ther no man

Swere and lyen, as a womman kan.

235   I sey nat this by wyves that been wyse,

But if it be whan they hem mysavyse.

A wys wyf, it that she kan hir good,

Shal beren hym on hond the cow is wood,

And take witnesse of hir owene mayde,

240   Of hir assent; but herkneth how I sayde.

  "Sir olde kaynard, is this thyn array?

Why is my neighebores wyf so gay?

She is honoured overal ther she gooth;

I sitte at hoom, I have no thrifty clooth.

245   What dostow at my neighebores hous?

Is she so fair? Artow so amorous?

What rowne ye with oure mayde? Benedicite,

Sir olde lecchour, lat thy japes be!

And if I have a gossib or a freend

250   Withouten gilt, thou chidest as a feend

If that I walke or pleye unto his hous.

Thou comest hoom as dronken as a mous

And prechest on thy bench, with yvel preef!

Thou seist to me, it is a greet meschief

The [prize of] bacon was not brought out for them, as I believe

That some [peaceful] men have [won] in Essex at Dunmowe.

225   *I governed them so well, by my own rules,*

That each of them was happy and eager,

To bring me fine things from the market.

They were very pleased when I spoke them pleasantly;

For God knows that I scolded them relentlessly.

230   *Now hear how well I conducted myself,*

You wise wives who know and understand.

Shall you thus speak and wrongly accuse them;

For there is no man who knows how to be half as barefaced

At swearing and lying as a woman knows.

235   *I say this not to those wives who are [already] wise,*

Except when they misadvise themselves.

A wise wife, if she knows her own good,

Shall convince him that the chough is mad,

And call her own maidservant as witness

240   *In agreement; but listen to how I spoke [to him].*

Sir old Slob, is this to be your treatment [of me]?

Why is my neighbour's wife so attractively dressed?

She is honoured wherever she goes;

I sit at home, I have no suitable clothes.

245   *What do you do at my neighbour's house?*

Is she so beautiful? Are you so amorous?

What do you whisper to our maidservant? Bless me!

Sir old Lecher, give up your deceit!

And if I have a confidant or a friend,

250   *Without any guilt, you will chide me like a devil*

If I walked to his house for [innocent] amusement.

You come home as drunk as a mouse,

And preach from your bench, curse you!

You say to me, it is a great misfortune,

255   To wedde a povre womman, for costage,

And if she be riche and of heigh parage,

Thanne seistow it is a tormentrie

To soffre hire pride and hir malencolie.

And if she be fair, thou verray knave,

260   Thou seyst that every holour wol hir have;

She may no while in chastitee abyde

That is assailled upon ech a syde.

Thou seyst, som folk desiren us for richesse,

Somme for oure shape, and somme for oure fairnesse,

265   And som for she kan outher synge or daunce,

And som for gentillesse and daliaunce,

Som for hir handes and hir armes smale;

Thus goth al to the devel by thy tale.

Thou seyst, men may nat kepe a castel wal,

270   It may so longe assailled been overal.

And if that she be foul, thou seist that she

Coveiteth every man that she may se;

For as a spaynel she wol on hym lepe

Til that she fynde som man hir to chepe;

275   Ne noon so grey goos gooth ther in the lake

As, seistow, wol been withoute make;

And seyst, it is an hard thyng for to welde

A thyng that no man wole, his thankes, helde.

Thus seistow, lorel, whan thow goost to bedde,

280   And that no wys man nedeth for to wedde,

Ne no man that entendeth unto hevene -

With wilde thonder-dynt and firy levene

Moote thy welked nekke be tobroke!

Thow seyst that droppyng houses, and eek smoke,

285   And chidyng wyves maken men to flee

Out of hir owene hous, a! benedicitee!

255 *To wed a poor woman due to the expense;*

And if she's rich and of higher birth,

Then you say it's a torment

To suffer her pride and moodiness.

And if she be beautiful, you utter peasant,

260 *You say that [because] every lecher will have her;*

She will not remain chaste for long

[When] she is harassed from every side.

You say, that some men desire us for our fortunes,

Some for our figures and some for our beauty:

265 *And some, because she knows how to sing or dance,*

And some, for noble birth and sociability;

Some for her hands and for her small arms;

Thus, by your tale, [we] all go to the devil.

You say men cannot defend a castle wall

270 *That has been attacked on all sides for a lengthy time.*

And if she is unattractive, you then say that she

Lusts after every man that she sees;

Leaping on him like a spaniel

Until she finds a man who will buy her;

275 *There's not one grey goose in the lake,*

As you tell it, that would be without a mate.

You say, it is a hard thing to control

Something that no man would willing keep

Thus, you say, scoundrel, when you go to bed;

280 *And that no wise man [thus] needs to marry,*

Nor a man who strives to enter Heaven.

[So] with furious thunder-claps and lightning

May your thin, withered neck be broken:

You say that leaking and also smoke-filled houses,

285 *And wives who scold, make men run away*

From their own house; ah, bless me!

What eyleth swich an old man for to chide?

Thow seyst, we wyves wol oure vices hide

Til we be fast, and thanne we wol hem shewe, -

290 Wel may that be a proverbe of a shrewe!

Thou seist, that oxen, asses, hors, and houndes,

They been assayd at diverse stoundes;

Bacyns, lavours, er that men hem bye,

Spoones and stooles, and al swich housbondrye,

295 And so been pottes, clothes, and array;

But folk of wyves maken noon assay

Til they be wedded, olde dotard shrewe!

And thanne, seistow, we wol oure vices shewe.

Thou seist also, that it displeseth me

300 But if that thou wolt preyse my beautee,

And but thou poure alwey upon my face,

And clepe me "faire dame" in every place,

And but thou make a feeste on thilke day

That I was born, and make me fressh and gay,

305 And but thou do to my norice honour,

And to my chamberere withinne my bour,

And to my fadres folk and hise allyes-

Thus seistow, olde barel-ful of lyes!

And yet of oure apprentice Janekyn,

310 For his crispe heer, shynynge as gold so fyn,

And for he squiereth me bothe up and doun,

Yet hastow caught a fals suspecioun.

I wol hym noght, thogh thou were deed tomorwe!

But tel me this, why hydestow, with sorwe,

315 The keyes of my cheste awey fro me?

It is my good as wel as thyn, pardee;

What, wenestow make an ydiot of oure dame?

Now by that lord that called is Seint Jame,

123

What afflicts such an old man to make him criticise so?

You say that we wives hide our vices

Until we are married, then we show them,

290   *That may well be the proverb of a scoundrel!*

You say that oxen, asses, horses and hounds ,

Have [all] been tested on various occasions;

Before men will buy basins, bowls,

And spoons and stools and all such household articles,

295   *And so with pots, clothes and preparation equipment;*

But men get no trial of their wives

Until they are married, old fool and scoundrel!

And then, you say, we show all our vices.

You say also that I am displeased

300   *Unless you praise and flatter my beauty,*

And constantly gaze always at my face

And call me "lovely lady" everywhere [we go];

And unless you make a feast on that day

When I was born, and give me pretty new clothes;

305   *And unless you show respect to my nurse*

As well as to my lady's maid in my bedroom,

And to my father's family and his friends-

So you say, old barrel full of lies!

And yet of our apprentice Jenkin,

310   *For his curly hair, shining like fine gold,*

And because he attends me continuously in every way,

You have been afflicted with a false suspicion;

I would give him nothing, even if you died tomorrow.

But tell me this, why do you hide, curse you,

315   *The keys to my strong-box away from me?*

By God, these are my goods as well as yours;

What, why would you make an idiot of the lady of the house?

Now by the lord who is called Saint James,

Thou shalt nat bothe, thogh that thou were wood,

320 Be maister of my body and of my good;

That oon thou shalt forgo, maugree thyne eyen.

What nedeth thee of me to enquere or spyen?

I trowe thou woldest loke me in thy chiste.

Thou sholdest seye, "Wyf, go wher thee liste,

325 Taak youre disport, I wol not leve no talys,

I knowe yow for a trewe wyf, dame Alys."

We love no man that taketh kepe or charge

Wher that we goon, we wol ben at our large.

Of alle men yblessed moot he be,

330 The wise astrologien, Daun Ptholome,

That seith this proverbe in his Almageste:

`Of alle men his wysdom is the hyeste,

That rekketh nevere who hath the world in honde.'

By this proverbe thou shalt understonde,

335 Have thou ynogh, what thar thee recche or care

How myrily that othere folkes fare?

For certeyn, olde dotard, by youre leve,

Ye shul have queynte right ynogh at eve.

He is to greet a nygard, that wolde werne

340 A man to lighte his candle at his lanterne;

He shal have never the lasse light, pardee,

Have thou ynogh, thee thar nat pleyne thee.

Thou seyst also, that if we make us gay

With clothyng and with precious array,

345 That it is peril of oure chastitee:

And yet, with sorwe, thou most enforce thee,

And seye thise wordes in the Apostles name,

"In habit, maad with chastitee and shame,

Ye wommen shul apparaille yow," quod he,

350 "And noght in tressed heer and gay perree,

You shall not have both, even if you scold like crazy;

320 [And] be master of both my body and my goods;

You must forego one, despite anything you can do.

Why do you need to make enquiries of me or spy?

I think you'd like to lock me in your chest!

You should say: "Wife, go wherever you like,

325 Have your fun, I will not believe any [malicious] tales;

I know you to be a good wife, lady Alison."

We love no man that watches over us or commands

Where we go, for we will be at liberty.

Of all men the most blessed may he be,

330 That wise astrologer, lord Ptolemy,

Who tells this proverb in his Almagest:

"The men with the highest wisdom,

Who cares nothing about who has control in the world."

By this proverb you shall understand:

335 [That] if you have enough, why are you concerned or care

How merrily all other folks live?

For certain, senile fool, by your leave,

You shall have plenty of my pleasing thing tonight.

He is too great a miser if he would refuse

340 To light a man's candle from his lantern

By God, he will never have any less light [for himself]

Since you have enough, there's nothing to complain about.

You also say that if we make ourselves attractive

With clothing, and with expensive adornments,

345 That it endangers our chastity;

Indeed, bad luck to you, you strengthen your stance

And repeat these words in St Paul's name:

"In clothing made for chastity, not shame,

You women shall dress yourselves," he said,

350 "And not with plaited hair, or jewellery,

As perles, ne with gold, ne clothes riche."

After thy text, ne after thy rubriche

I wol nat wirche, as muchel as a gnat!

Thou seydest this, that I was lyk a cat;

355 For whoso wolde senge a cattes skyn,

Thanne wolde the cat wel dwellen in his in.

And if the cattes skyn be slyk and gay,

She wol nat dwelle in house half a day,

But forth she wole, er any day be dawed,

360 To shewe hir skyn, and goon a-caterwawed.

This is to seye, if I be gay, sire shrewe,

I wol renne out, my borel for to shewe.

Sire olde fool, what eyleth thee to spyen,

Thogh thou preye Argus, with his hundred eyen,

365 To be my warde-cors, as he kan best,

In feith, he shal nat kepe me but me lest;

Yet koude I make his berd, so moot I thee.

Thou seydest eek, that ther been thynges thre,

The whiche thynges troublen al this erthe,

370 And that no wight ne may endure the ferthe.

O leeve sire shrewe, Jesu shorte thy lyf!

Yet prechestow, and seyst an hateful wyf

Yrekened is for oon of thise meschances.

Been ther none othere maner resemblances

375 That ye may likne youre parables to,

But if a sely wyf be oon of tho?

Thou likenest wommenes love to helle,

To bareyne lond, ther water may nat dwelle.

Thou liknest it also to wilde fyr;

380 The moore it brenneth, the moore it hath desir

To consume every thyng that brent wole be.

Thou seyest, right as wormes shende a tree,

Like pearls, nor with gold, or expensive gowns;"

About your text and your interpretation

I will not follow them any more than I would a gnat.

You said this, that I was like a cat;

355   For whoever would singe a cat's fur,

Then the cat would remain inside the house;

And if the cat's coat be all sleek and beautiful,

She will not stay in the house even half a day,

But she will go out, before the dawn of any day,

360   To show her fur and caterwaul and play.

This is to say, Sir Scoundrel, if I'm finely dressed,

I would run out to show my clothes.

Sir old fool, what afflicts you to spy [on me]?

Though you ask Argus, with his hundred eyes,

365   To be my body-guard, as he knows best,

In faith, he shall not watch me, unless I am willing;

Yet, I could deceive him - trust me!

You also say, that there are three things-

Which are a trouble on this earth,

370   And that no person could endure the fourth:

O dear Sir Rogue, may Christ cut short your life!

Yet you preach and say that a hateful wife

Is reckoned to be one of those misfortunes.

[But] are there no other kinds of comparisons

375   That you could use as an analogy in your parables,

Unless [using] an innocent wife is one of them??

You liken women's love to Hell,

To desert land where water does not collect.

You also liken it to [inextinguishable] Greek fire;

380   The more it burns, the more it craves

To consume everything that can be burned.

You say that just as worms destroy a tree,

Right so a wyf destroyeth hir housbond.

This knowe they, that been to wyves bonde."

385   Lordynges, right thus, as ye have understonde,

Baar I stifly myne olde housbondes on honde,

That thus they seyden in hir dronkenesse;

And al was fals, but that I took witnesse

On Janekyn and on my nece also.

390   O lord! The pyne I dide hem, and the wo

Ful giltelees, by Goddes sweete pyne!

For as an hors I koude byte and whyne,

I koude pleyne, thogh I were in the gilt,

Or elles often tyme hadde I been spilt.

395   Who so that first to mille comth first grynt;

I pleyned first, so was oure werre ystynt.

They were ful glad to excuse hem ful blyve

Of thyng of which they nevere agilte hir lyve.

Of wenches wolde I beren hym on honde,

400   Whan that for syk unnethes myghte he stonde,

Yet tikled it his herte, for that he!

Wende that I hadde of hym so greet chiertee.

I swoor that al my walkynge out by nyghte

Was for t'espye wenches that he dighte.

405   Under that colour hadde I many a myrthe;

For al swich wit is yeven us in oure byrthe,

Deceite, wepyng, spynnyng, God hath yive

To wommen kyndely whil they may lyve.

And thus of o thyng I avaunte me,

410   Atte ende I hadde the bettre in ech degree,

By sleighte, or force, or by som maner thyng,

As by continueel murmur or grucchyng.

Namely a bedde hadden they meschaunce;

Ther wolde I chide and do hem no plesaunce,

Does a wife subject her husband to hardship;

Men who that are bound to their wives know this

385 *Gentlemen, as you have understood, in this very way,*

I resolutely swore that my old husbands

Had said these things in their drunkenness;

[But] all of this was a lie, but I brought the witness

Of jenkin and of my dear niece also.

390 *O Lord, the pain and the misery I caused them,*

[Yet] by God's suffering, they were innocent!

For like a stallion I could bite and neigh.

Although the guilt was all mine, I could complain,

If not, there were many times when I would have been done for.

395 *For whoever come to the mill first, grinds first*

I complained first, so our war was ended.

They were very happy to excuse themselves very quickly

For something they had never done in their lives.

I would accuse him of [going] with young girls,

400 *When, due to sickness, he could hardly stand.*

Yet it tickled his heart, since he thereby

Believed that I had great love for him.

I swore that my wandering about at night

Was to spy on girls with whom he was having sex;

405 *Under that pretence I had a lot of fun;*

For all such skills are given to us at birth;

Deceit, weeping, spinning skills , God has given

To women, naturally, for their whole lives.

And thus of one thing I can boast,

410 *In the end, I got the best of each of them,*

By trick, or force, or by some such device,

Such as by constant complaints or grumbling;

Especially if they suffered a misfortune in bed,

I would then scold them and give them no pleasure;

415   I wolde no lenger in the bed abyde,

           If that I felte his arm over my syde

           Til he had maad his raunsoun unto me;

           Thanne wolde I suffre hym do his nycetee.

           And therfore every man this tale I telle,

420   Wynne who so may, for al is for to selle;

           With empty hand men may none haukes lure.

           For wynnyng wolde I al his lust endure

           And make me a feyned appetit;

           And yet in bacon hadde I nevere delit;

425   That made me that evere I wolde hem chide.

           For thogh the pope hadde seten hem biside,

           I wolde nat spare hem at hir owene bord,

           For by my trouthe I quitte hem word for word.

           As help me verray God omnipotent,

430   Though I right now sholde make my testament,

           I ne owe hem nat a word, that it nys quit.

           I broghte it so aboute by my wit,

           That they moste yeve it up as for the beste,

           Or elles hadde we nevere been in reste.

435   For thogh he looked as a wood leon,

           Yet sholde he faille of his conclusioun.

           Thanne wolde I seye, "Goode lief, taak keep,

           How mekely looketh Wilkyn oure sheep!

           Com neer, my spouse, lat me ba thy cheke!

440   Ye sholde been al pacient and meke,

           And han a sweete spiced conscience,

           Sith ye so preche of Jobes pacience.

           Suffreth alwey, syn ye so wel kan preche,

           And but ye do, certein we shal yow teche

445   That it is fair to have a wyf in pees.

           Oon of us two moste bowen, doutelees;

415   I would not stay in the bed any longer

If I felt his arm across my side,

Until he had paid his ransom to me;

Then would I let him satisfy his lust.

And, therefore, to all men I will tell this tale,

420   Everyone can win, for everything is up for sale.

Men cannot lure a hawk with an empty hand;

To make profit, I would endure his lust.

And pretend to have a sexual desire;

Yet I have never taken pleasure from old meat;

425   And that is why I used to scold so much.

For even if the pope was sitting beside them

I would not have spared them, even at their own table,

For by my truth, I paid them back, word for word.

So help me, the true omnipotent God,

430   If I was to make my will right away,

I would owe them not one word that has not been repaid.

So, by my cunning, I brought it about,

That they were forced to give up, as their best choice,

Or otherwise we would never have had rest.

435   For although he looked like a mad lion,

He would still fail to achieve his wishes.

Then would I say: 'My dear, take heed

Of how meek Willie, our old sheep, looks;

Come near, my spouse, let me kiss your cheek!

440   You should always be patient and meek,

And have a pleasing disposition,

Since you preach so about Job's patience,

Suffer always, since you know how to preach so well;

And, unless you do, [you can] be sure that we'll teach

445   That it is desirable to have a peaceful wife.

Certainly, one of us two must yield,

And sith a man is moore resonable,

Than womman is, ye moste been suffrable."

What eyleth yow to grucche thus and grone?

450   Is it for ye wolde have my queynte allone?

Wy, taak it al! lo, have it every deel!

Peter! I shrewe yow, but ye love it weel;

For if I wolde selle my bele chose,

I koude walke as fressh as is a rose

455   But I wol kepe it for youre owene tooth.

Ye be to blame, by God! I sey yow sooth."

Swiche manere wordes hadde we on honde.

Now wol I speken of my fourthe housbonde.

My fourthe housbonde was a revelour -

460   This is to seyn, he hadde a paramour -

And I was yong and ful of ragerye,

Stibourn and strong, and joly as a pye.

Wel koude I daunce to an harpe smale,

And synge, ywis, as any nyghtyngale,

465   Whan I had dronke a draughte of sweete wyn.

Metellius, the foule cherl, the swyn,

That with a staf birafte his wyf hire lyf,

For she drank wyn, thogh I hadde been his wyf,

He sholde nat han daunted me fro drynke.

470   And after wyn on Venus moste I thynke,

For al so siker as cold engendreth hayl,

A likerous mouth moste han a likerous tayl.

In wommen vinolent is no defence,

This knowen lecchours by experience.

475   But, Lord Crist! whan that it remembreth me

Upon my yowthe and on my jolitee,

It tikleth me aboute myn herte roote.

Unto this day it dooth myn herte boote

And since a man is more reasonable,

Than is a woman, you are most able to endure hardship.

What afflicts you that you grumble and groan in such a way?

450   *Is it because you want my vagina all to yourself?*

Okay take it all. Look, have every bit of it;

By St Peter! I would curse you if you didn't love it so much!

For if I was to sell my beautiful thing,

I could walk out as fresh as a rose;

455   *But I will keep it all for you.*

You are to blame, by God! I tell the truth

Such were the manner of words we had [between us].

.'   *Now will I tell you about my fourth husband.*

My fourth husband was a reveler,

460   *That is to say, he kept a mistress;*

Then, I was young and full of passion,

Stubborn and strong and as chatty as a magpie.

I could dance very well to a small harp,

And sing as well as any nightingale,

465   *When I had drunk a draught of sweet wine.*

Metellius, the foul peasant. the swine,

Killed his wife with a staff,

Because she had drunk wine, although If I had been his wife,

He would never have frightened me away from drink;

470   *For after wine, I always think of Venus,*

For just as surely as cold produces hail,

A gluttonous mouth must have a lecherous tail

In women, drunkenness is not a defence,

This all lechers know by experience.

475   *But Lord Christ! When I remember*

My youth and my gaiety ,

It tickles me to the bottom of my heart

Right up to today, my heart sings in salute

That I have had my world, as in my tyme.
480 But age, allas, that al wole envenyme,
Hath me biraft my beautee and my pith!
Lat go, farewel, the devel go therwith!
The flour is goon, ther is namoore to telle,
The bren as I best kan, now moste I selle;
485 But yet to be right myrie wol I fonde.
Now wol I tellen of my fourthe housbonde.
I seye, I hadde in herte greet despit
That he of any oother had delit;
But he was quit, by God and by Seint Joce!
490 I made hym of the same wode a croce;
Nat of my body in no foul manere,
But certeinly, I made folk swich cheere
That in his owene grece I made hym frye
For angre and for verray jalousye.
495 By God, in erthe I was his purgatorie,
For which I hope his soule be in glorie,
For, God it woot, he sat ful ofte and song
Whan that his shoo ful bitterly hym wrong!
Ther was no wight save God and he, that wiste
500 In many wise how soore I hym twiste.
He deyde whan I cam fro Jerusalem,
And lith ygrave under the roode-beem,
Al is his tombe noght so curyus
As was the sepulcre of hym Daryus,
505 Which that Appelles wroghte subtilly.
It nys but wast to burye hym preciously,
Lat hym fare-wel, God yeve his soule reste,
He is now in his grave, and in his cheste.
Now of my fifthe housbonde wol I telle.
510 God lete his soule nevere come in helle!

135

That, in my lifetime, I have had the world.

480   *But age which, alas, poisons everything,*

Has taken away my beauty and my vigour;

Let it go! Farewell! And may the devil go with it!

The flour is gone, there is no more to tell,

I must now hawk around the rough bran as best as I know how;

485   *But I will try to be very merry and*

Will now tell you about my fourth husband.

I say that I had great anger in my heart

When he enjoyed himself with another woman.

But God and by Saint Judocus paid him back!

490   *I made him a cross of that same wood [he had used against me];*

But not with my body in a disgusting way,

But truly, I was so cheery with other folk

That I made him fry in his own grease

For [my] anger and for true jealousy.

495   *By God, I was his purgatory on Earth,*

For which I hope his soul now lives in glory,

For God knows, many a time he sat and cried out

When his shoe pinched him badly.

There was no person, save God and he, who knew

500   *How, in so many ways, I would torture him.*

He died when I returned from Jerusalem,

And lies entombed before the great chancel screen,

Although his tomb is not so lavish

As was Darius' grave,

505   *Which Apelles built so skilfully;*

It was nothing but waste to bury him expensively.

Let him fare well. God give his soul good rest,

He is now in his grave, in his coffin.

I will now tell you about my fifth husband.

510   *May God ensure his soul never goes to Hell!*

And yet was he to me the mooste shrewe;

That feele I on my ribbes al by rewe,

And evere shal, unto myn endyng day.

But in oure bed he was ful fressh and gay,

515 And therwithal so wel koude he me glose

Whan that he solde han my *bele chose*,

That thogh he hadde me bet on every bon

He koude wynne agayn my love anon.

I trowe I loved hym beste, for that he

520 Was of his love daungerous to me.

We wommen han, if that I shal nat lye,

In this matere a queynte fantasye;

Wayte what thyng we may nat lightly have,

Therafter wol we crie al day and crave.

525 Forbede us thyng, and that desiren we;

Preesse on us faste, and thanne wol we fle;

With daunger oute we al oure chaffare.

Greet prees at market maketh deere ware,

And to greet cheep is holde at litel prys;

530 This knoweth every womman that is wys.

My fifthe housbonde, God his soule blesse,

Which that I took for love and no richesse,

He somtyme was a clerk of Oxenford,

And hadde left scole, and wente at hom to bord

535 With my gossib, dwellynge in oure toun,

God have hir soule! hir name was Alisoun.

She knew myn herte and eek my privetee

Bet than oure parisshe preest, as moot I thee.

To hir biwreyed I my conseil al,

540 For hadde myn housbonde pissed on a wal,

Or doon a thyng that sholde han cost his lyf,

To hir, and to another worthy wyf,

137

And yet he was also the most brutal to me;

I can still feel the pain in each rib, one after the other,

And shall always do so, until my dying day.

But in our bed he was very lively and jovial,

515 *And, furthermore, he knew very well how to talk me round,*

Whenever he wanted my beautiful thing,

That although he had beaten every bone of my body,

He could re-win my love very quickly.

I believe I loved him best of all, for he

520 *Was very sparing when giving his love to me.*

I shall not lie, we women have,

A peculiar fantasy in love matters;

We look out for whatever things we cannot easily have,

And thereafter we will cry all day and crave for it.

525 *Forbid us something, and we will desire it more;*

[But] force a thing on us and then we will run away.

Women lay out our desirable wares only reluctantly,

{For] great crowds at the market make goods dearer,

And what is too abundant commands a low price;

530 *Every wise woman knows this.*

My fifth husband, may God bless his spirit!

Whom I took for love, and not riches,

Had been sometime a student at Oxford,

And had left college and came home to lodge

535 *With my best friend, who lived in our town,*

God save her soul! Her name was Alison.

She knew my heart and all my secrets

Better than our parish priest, I must say.

I confided all my secrets to her.

540 *For if my husband had pissed against a wall,*

Or had done a thing that could have cost him his life,

To her and to another worthy wife,

And to my nece, which that I loved weel,

I wolde han toold his conseil every deel.

545 And so I dide ful often, God it woot,

That made his face ful often reed and hoot

For verray shame, and blamed hym-self, for he

Had toold to me so greet a pryvetee.

And so bifel that ones, in a Lente -

550 So often tymes I to my gossyb wente,

For evere yet I loved to be gay,

And for to walke in March, Averill, and May,

Fro hous to hous to heere sondry talys -

That Jankyn Clerk and my gossyb, dame Alys,

555 And I myself into the feeldes wente.

Myn housbonde was at London al that Lente;

I hadde the bettre leyser for to pleye,

And for to se, and eek for to be seye

Of lusty folk; what wiste I, wher my grace

560 Was shapen for to be, or in what place?

Therfore I made my visitaciouns

To vigilies and to processiouns,

To prechyng eek, and to thise pilgrimages,

To pleyes of myracles, and to mariages;

565 And wered upon my gaye scarlet gytes.

Thise wormes ne thise motthes, ne thise mytes,

Upon my peril, frete hem never a deel;

And wostow why? for they were used weel!

Now wol I tellen forth what happed me.

570 I seye, that in the feeldes walked we,

Til trewely we hadde swich daliance,

This clerk and I, that of my purveiance

I spak to hym, and seyde hym, how that he,

If I were wydwe, sholde wedde me.

139

And to my niece whom I have always loved,

I would have told his secrets in every detail,

545   *And, God knows, I did so many times,*

Which often made his face become very red and hot

Out of true shame, and blamed himself that he

Had told me such a great secret.

So, it happened one day in Lent

550   *For I often went to visit my closest friend,*

Since I always loved to be happy and jolly

And during March, April, and May, to go walking

From house to house, to hear the latest gossip

That Jenkin the secretary, and my best friend lady Alice,

555   *And myself went into the meadows.*

My husband was in London for all of that Lent;

I had a better chance to play,

And to watch, and to be seen

By lusty folk; What did I know what my fate

560   *Was destined to be, or in what place?*

Therefore, I made my visits

To vigils and religious processions,

Listening to preachers also, and to sites of pilgrimage,

To watch miracle plays, and to marriages,

565   *And wore my pretty scarlet dresses.*

The worms nor the moths nor the mites,

Never ate into them, I swear;

And do you know why? For they were used so often!

Now will I tell you what happened to me.

570   *I say that we three walked in the meadows,*

Until, truly, we became very flirtatious,

This learned man and I, that with thoughts of my future provision,

I spoke to him and told him that he,

If I was to become a widow, should marry me.

575	For certeinly, I sey for no bobance,
	Yet was I nevere withouten purveiance
	Of mariage, n'of othere thynges eek.
	I holde a mouses herte nat worth a leek
	That hath but oon hole for to sterte to,
580	And if that faille, thanne is al ydo.
	I bar hym on honde, he hadde enchanted me, -
	My dame taughte me that soutiltee.
	And eek I seyde, I mette of hym al nyght,
	He wolde han slayn me as I lay upright,
585	And al my bed was ful of verray blood;
	But yet I hope that he shal do me good,
	For blood bitokeneth gold, as me was taught-
	And al was fals, I dremed of it right naught,
	But as I folwed ay my dames loore
590	As wel of this, as of othere thynges moore.
	But now sir, lat me se, what I shal seyn?
	A ha, by God, I have my tale ageyn.
	Whan that my fourthe housbonde was on beere,
	I weep algate, and made sory cheere,
595	As wyves mooten, for it is usage-
	And with my coverchief covered my visage;
	But for that I was purveyed of a make,
	I wepte but smal, and that I undertake.
	To chirche was myn housbonde born amorwe
600	With neighebores that for hym maden sorwe;
	And Janekyn oure clerk was oon of tho.
	As help me God! whan that I saugh hym go
	After the beere, me thoughte he hadde a paire
	Of legges and of feet so clene and faire,
605	That al myn herte I yaf unto his hoold.
	He was, I trowe, a twenty wynter oold,

575	For certainly, I do not mean to boast,
	But I was never without propositions
	Of marriage, nor of other things as well.
	I hold a mouse's life is worth nothing
	[If] he has only one hole into which he can run,
580	And if that [hole] fails, then he is done.
	I falsely accused him that he had enchanted me;-
	My mother taught me that trick.
	And I also said I'd dreamed about him all night,
	He would have killed me as I lay on my back,
585	And that my bed was full of blood;
	But yet, I hoped that he would do me good,
	For I was taught that blood represents gold-
	[Yet] all of this was a lie, I never dreamed about this,
	But I followed my mother's teaching
590	On this matter, as well as on many more things.
	But now, sir, let me see, what was I going to say?
	Aha, by God, I know! I have my tale to tell.
	When my fourth husband lay dead in his coffin,
	I wept continuously, and had a sorrowful expression,
595	As wives must always do, for it is the custom,
	And I covered my face with a veil;
	But since I was provided with a mate,
	I can say that I wept only a little.
	My husband was carried to church the next morning
600	By neighbours that who mourned for him;
	And our Jenkin our secretary, was one of them.
	So help me God, when I saw him
	Follow the coffin, I thought he had a pair
	Of legs and feet so neat and attractive
605	That I gave him all my heart to hold.
	He was, I think, twenty winters old,

And I was fourty, if I shal seye sooth,

But yet I hadde alwey a coltes tooth.

Gat-tothed I was, and that bicam me weel,

610   I hadde the prente of Seinte Venus seel.

As help me God, I was a lusty oon,

And faire, and riche, and yong, and wel bigon,

And trewely, as myne housbondes tolde me,

I hadde the beste *quonyam* myghte be.

615   For certes, I am al Venerien

In feelynge, and myn herte is Marcien.

Venus me yaf my lust, my likerousnesse,

And Mars yaf me my sturdy hardynesse.

Myn ascendent was Taur, and Mars therinne,

620   Allas, allas, that evere love was synne!

I folwed ay myn inclinacioun

By vertu of my constellacioun;

That made me I koude noght withdrawe

My chambre of Venus from a good felawe.

625   Yet have I Martes mark upon my face,

And also in another privee place.

For God so wys be my savacioun,

I ne loved nevere by no discrecioun,

But evere folwede myn appetit,

630   Al were he short, or long, or blak, or whit.

I took no kep, so that he liked me,

How poore he was, ne eek of what degree.

What sholde I seye, but at the monthes ende

This joly clerk Jankyn, that was so hende

635   Hath wedded me with greet solempnytee,

And to hym yaf I al the lond and fee

That evere was me yeven therbifoore;

But afterward repented me ful soore;

And I was forty, if I am to tell the truth;

But then I always had the appetite for the young.

Gap-toothed I was, and that suited me well;

610 *I had the print of holy Venus' seal.*

So help me God, I was a lively one,

And fair and rich and young and well-off;

And truly, as my husbands all told me,

I had the best belle chose there could be.

615 *For certain, I am of Venus*

emotionally, whilst my character is of Mars.

Venus gave me my lust, my wantonness,

And Mars gave me my obstinate boldness.

[On my birth] Taurus was in ascendance, with Mars therein,

620 *Alas, alas, that ever love was [considered] a sin!*

I always followed my inclination

By virtue of my star sign;

Which made me so that I could never refuse

My love-chamber from a good fellow.

625 *Yet have I a red mark upon my face,*

And also in another private place.

For as God, so wise, will be my salvation,

have never loved in moderation,

But have always followed my own appetite,

630 *Whether he was short or tall, or black or white;*

I took no heed, so long that he pleasured me,

How poor he was, nor even of what rank.

What should I say, save, at the month's end,

This jolly secretary Jenkin, that was so handsome

635 *Had married me with full ceremony,*

And to him I gave all the land absolutely

That had ever been given to me beforehand;

But later, I was bitterly regretful.

He nolde suffre nothyng of my list.

640 By God, he smoot me ones on the lyst

For that I rente out of his book a leef,

That of the strook myn ere wax al deef.

Stibourne I was as is a leonesse,

And of my tonge a verray jangleresse,

645 And walke I wolde, as I had doon biforn,

From hous to hous, although he had it sworn,

For which he often-tymes wolde preche,

And me of olde Romayn geestes teche,

How he Symplicius Gallus lefte his wyf,

650 And hir forsook for terme of al his lyf,

Noght but for open-heveded he hir say,

Lookynge out at his dore, upon a day.

Another Romayn tolde he me by name,

That for his wyf was at a someres game

655 Withoute his wityng, he forsook hir eke.

And thanne wolde he upon his Bible seke

That like proverbe of Ecclesiaste,

Where he comandeth, and forbedeth faste,

Man shal nat suffre his wyf go roule aboute,

660 Thanne wolde he seye right thus, withouten doute:

"Who so that buyldeth his hous al of salwes,

And priketh his blynde hors over the falwes,

And suffreth his wyf to go seken halwes,

Is worthy to been hanged on the galwes!"

665 But al for noght, I sette noght an hawe

Of his proverbes, n'of his olde sawe,

Ne I wolde nat of hym corrected be.

I hate hym that my vices telleth me;

And so doo mo, God woot, of us than I.

670 This made hym with me wood al outrely,

He never allowed me to have my wishes.

640 *By God, he struck me once on the ear,*

Because I tore a page from out of his book,

From that strike my ear became completely deaf.

I was as stubborn as a lioness,

And with my tongue like a true chatterbox,

645 *I would walk, as I had done before,*

From house to house, although he had sworn that I should not.

For which he would often preach

And lecture me about old Roman tales,

How a man called Symplicius Gallus left his wife

650 *And abandoned her for the rest of his life*

For nothing more than her going bare-headed, he said

[When] looking out of his door one day.

He told me about another Roman, by name,

Who, because his wife was at a summer festivity

655 *Without him knowing, he also abandoned her.*

And then he would search inside his Bible for

That proverb of Ecclesiasticus

Where he commanded, and strictly forbade,

That a man should suffer his wife to go gadding about;

660 *He would then say as follows, without doubt:*

> *"Whosoever that builds his house out of sallows,*
>
> *And spurs his blind horse over the fallows,*
>
> *And allows his wife to go alone seeking hallows,*
>
> *Is worthy to be hanged upon the gallows."*

665 *But that was all for nothing, I had no regard*

For his proverbs, nor for his old sayings,

Nor yet would I be corrected by him.

I hate someone who tells me about my shortcomings;

God knows, and so do more of us than just myself.

670 *This made him insanely angry with me,*

I nolde noght forbere hym in no cas.

Now wol I seye yow sooth, by seint Thomas,

Why that I rente out of his book a leef,

For which he smoot me so that I was deef.

675   He hadde a book that gladly, nyght and day,

For his desport he wolde rede alway.

He cleped it Valerie and Theofraste,

At whiche book he lough alwey ful faste.

And eek ther was som tyme a clerk at Rome,

680   A cardinal that highte Seint Jerome,

That made a book agayn Jovinian,

In whiche book eek ther was Tertulan,

Crisippus, Trotula, and Helowys,

That was abbesse nat fer fro Parys,

685   And eek the Parables of Salomon,

Ovides Art, and bookes many on,

And alle thise were bounden in o volume,

And every nyght and day was his custume

Whan he hadde leyser and vacacioun

690   From oother worldly occupacioun

To reden on this book of wikked wyves.

He knew of hem mo legendes and lyves

Than been of goode wyves in the Bible.

For trusteth wel, it is an impossible

695   That any clerk wol speke good of wyves,

But if it be of hooly seintes lyves,

Ne of noon oother womman never the mo.

Who peyntede the leon, tel me, who?

By God! if wommen hadde writen stories,

700   As clerkes han withinne hire oratories,

They wolde han writen of men moore wikkednesse

Than all the mark of Adam may redresse.

[But] in no event would I not submit to him.

Now, by Saint Thomas, I will tell you the truth,

About why I tore a leaf out of his book,

For which he struck me so that I became deaf.

675 *He had a book that happily, night and day,*

He would always read for his amusement.

He called it 'Valerius' and 'Theophrastus',

At which book he would always laugh most heartily.

And also, there once was a cleric at Rome,

680 *A cardinal, that was called Saint Jerome,*

Who made a book against Jovinian;

In which book, too, there was also Tertullian,

Chrysippus, Trotula, and Heloise

Who was an abbess not far from Paris;

685 *And also the Proverbs of King Solomon,*

Ovid's Art, and many other books.

And all these were bound in one volume.

And every night and day it was his custom,

When he had leisure and free time

690 *From all his other worldly occupation,*

To read, this book about wicked wives.

He knew more of those legends and lives

Than of all the good wives contained in the Bible.

For trust me, it is an impossibility,

695 *That any cleric will speak well of wives,*

Unless it is about the holy saints' lives,

But never of any other women.

Who first painted the lion? Tell me, who?

By God, if women had written stories,

700 *As the scholars have within their study rooms,*

They would have written more about men's wickedness

Than all the male gender could redress.

The children of Mercurie and Venus

Been in hir wirkyng ful contrarius,

705 Mercurie loveth wysdam and science,

And Venus loveth ryot and dispence.

And for hire diverse disposicioun

Ech falleth in otheres exaltacioun,

And thus, God woot, Mercurie is desolat

710 In Pisces, wher Venus is exaltat;

And Venus falleth ther Mercurie is reysed.

Therfore no womman of no clerk is preysed.

The clerk, whan he is oold and may noght do

Of Venus werkes worth his olde sho,

715 Thanne sit he doun, and writ in his dotage

That wommen kan nat kepe hir mariage.

But now to purpos, why I tolde thee

That I was beten for a book, pardee.

Upon a nyght Jankyn, that was oure sire,

720 Redde on his book as he sat by the fire

Of Eva first, that for hir wikkednesse

Was al mankynde broght to wrecchednesse,

For which that Jhesu Crist hymself was slayn,

That boghte us with his herte blood agayn.

725 Lo, heere expres of womman may ye fynde,

That womman was the los of al mankynde.

Tho redde he me how Sampson loste hise heres,

Slepynge, his lemman kitte it with hir sheres,

Thurgh whiche tresoun loste he bothe hise yen.

730 Tho redde he me, if that I shal nat lyen,

Of Hercules and of his Dianyre,

That caused hym to sette hymself afyre.

No thyng forgat he the penaunce and wo

That Socrates hadde with hise wyves two,

The children of Mercury [scholars] and Venus [lovers]

Are directly opposite in their actions,

705   For Mercury loves wisdom and knowledge,

And Venus loves revelry and extravagance.

And [because] of their different natures,

Each falls when the other is in ascendance.

And thus, God knows, Mercury is helpless and powerless

710   In Pisces, where Venus is exalted;

And Venus falls when Mercury rises;

Therefore, no woman is praised by a cleric.

[Yet] the cleric, when he is old and cannot do [any]

Of Venus' work worth his worn-out shoe,

715   Then, he sits down and writes in his old age

That women do not know how to keep their marriage vows.

But now [back] to the point, why I told you

That, by God, I was beaten for a book.

One night, Jenkin, the master of our household,

720   Read in his book, as he sat by the fire

About the Eve who, by her wickedness, first

Brought all mankind to wretchedness,

For which Lord Jesus Christ Himself was slain,

That again redeemed us with His heart's blood.

725   Lo here, you can find it expressly said of woman,

That woman was the ruin of all mankind.

Then he read to me about how Samson lost his hair,

[While] sleeping, his lover cut it with her shears;

By reason of this treason he lost both of his eyes.

730   Then he read to me, no word of a lie,

Of Hercules, and his [wife] Deianira

Who caused him to set himself on fire.

Nor did he forget the suffering and woe

That Socrates had with his two wives;

735	How Xantippa caste pisse upon his heed.
	This sely man sat stille as he were deed;
	He wiped his heed, namoore dorste he seyn
	But, "Er that thonder stynte, comth a reyn."
	Of Phasipha, that was the queene of Crete,
740	For shrewednesse hym thoughte the tale swete-
	Fy! Speke namoore - it is a grisly thyng -
	Of hir horrible lust and hir likyng.
	Of Clitermystra for hire lecherye,
	That falsly made hir housbonde for to dye,
745	He redde it with ful good devocioun.
	He tolde me eek for what occasioun
	Amphiorax at Thebes loste his lyf.
	Myn housbonde hadde a legende of his wyf
	Eriphilem, that for an ouche of gold
750	Hath prively unto the Grekes told
	Wher that hir housbonde hidde hym in a place,
	For which he hadde at Thebes sory grace.
	Of Lyvia tolde he me, and of Lucye,
	They bothe made hir housbondes for to dye,
755	That oon for love, that oother was for hate.
	Lyvia hir housbonde, on an even late,
	Empoysoned hath, for that she was his fo.
	Lucia, likerous, loved hir housbonde so,
	That for he sholde alwey upon hire thynke,
760	She yaf hym swich a manere love-drynke
	That he was deed, er it were by the morwe.
	And thus algates housbondes han sorw.
	Thanne tolde he me, how that Latumyus
	Compleyned unto his felawe Arrius,
765	That in his gardyn growed swich a tree,
	On which he seyde how that hise wyves thre

151

735   *How Xantippe threw urine over his head;*

           This hapless man sat still, as if he were dead;

           He wiped his head, daring to say no more

           Except 'before the thunder ceases, comes the rain.'

           Of Pasiphae, who was the queen of Crete [who copulated with a bull],

740   *For depravity, he thought the story was pleasing-*

           Fie! Speak no more- it is a disgusting thing -

           About her horrible lust and her sexual desires.

           Of Clytemnystra, for her lechery,

           That wrongly caused her husband's death,

745   *He read it with great interest,.*

           He also told me the cause why

           Amphiaraus lost his life at Thebes;

           My husband had a story about his wife

           Eriphyle, who, for a gold brooch,

750   *Secretly told the Greeks*

           Where her husband had his hiding place,

           For which he met a sorry fate at Thebes.

           Of Livia and Lucie he told me,

           Both caused their husbands to die,

755   *One for love, the other for hate.*

           Late one evening, For her husband, Livia

           Made him a poisoned drink, for she was his enemy.

           Lucia, so amorous, had such love for her husband

           So that he would always think about her

760   *She gave him such a form of love-potion,*

           That he was dead before the morning;

           And thus, in either case, husbands came to sorrow.

           Then did he tell how one Latumius

           Complained to his friend Arrius,

765   *That in his garden there grew such a tree*

           On which, he said, his three wives,

Hanged hemself, for herte despitus.

"O leeve brother," quod this Arrius,

"Yif me a plante of thilke blissed tree,

770 And in my gardyn planted it shal bee."

Of latter date of wyves hath he red,

That somme han slayn hir housbondes in hir bed,

And lete hir lecchour dighte hir al the nyght,

Whan that the corps lay in the floor upright.

775 And somme han dryve nayles in hir brayn

Whil that they slepte, and thus they han hem slayn.

Somme han hem yeve poysoun in hir drynke.

He spak moore harm than herte may bithynke,

And therwithal he knew of mo proverbes

780 Than in this world ther growen gras or herbes.

"Bet is," quod he, "thyn habitacioun

Be with a leon, or a foul dragoun,

Than with a womman usynge for to chyde."

"Bet is," quod he, "hye in the roof abyde

785 Than with an angry wyf doun in the hous,

They been so wikked and contrarious.

They haten that hir housbondes loveth ay."

He seyde, "a womman cast hir shame away

Whan she cast of hir smok," and forther mo,

790 "A fair womman, but she be chaast also,

Is lyk a goldryng in a sowes nose."

Who wolde leeve, or who wolde suppose

The wo that in myn herte was, and pyne?

And whan I saugh he wolde nevere fyne

795 To reden on this cursed book al nyght,

Al sodeynly thre leves have I plyght

Out of his book, right as he radde, and eke

I with my fest so took hym on the cheke,

Had hanged themselves with a spiteful heart.

"O dear brother,' this Arrius said,

Give me a graft from that same blessed tree

770 *And it shall be planted in my garden!'*

He read about wives in later times,

That some had killed their husbands in their bed,

And let their lovers have sex with them all night

While [their husband's] corpse lay face up on the floor.

775 *And some had nails driven into their brain*

While they slept, and thus had them killed.

Some had given them poison in their drink.

He spoke more evil than the heart can imagine.

And moreover, he knew of more proverbs

780 *Than there is grass or herbs growing in this world.*

"It is better," he said, "that your dwelling is [shared]

With a lion or a hideous dragon,",

"Than with a woman who is accustomed to scolding."

"It is better," he said, "to live high on the roof

785 *Than with an angry wife down in the house,*

They are so wicked and contrary,

They hate anything their husband loves, for sure."

He said, "a woman throws her shame away

When she takes off her undergarments," and furthermore,

790 *"An attractive woman, unless she is also chaste,*

Is like a gold ring in a pig's nose."

Who would imagine, or who would suppose

What grief and pain there was in my heart?

And when I saw he would never stop

795 *Reading this cursed book all night,*

Without warning, I pulled three leaves

Out of his book, as he read, and also

I struck him on the cheek with my fist,

That in oure fyr he ril bakward adoun.

800   And he up-stirte as dooth a wood leoun,

And with his fest he smoot me on the heed

That in the floor I lay, as I were deed.

And whan he saugh how stille that I lay,

He was agast, and wolde han fled his way,

805   Til atte laste out of my swogh I breyde.

'O, hastow slayn me, false theef,' I seyde,

'And for my land thus hastow mordred me?

Er I be deed, yet wol I kisse thee.'

And neer he cam and kneled faire adoun,

810   And seyde, 'Deere suster Alisoun,

As help me God, I shal thee nevere smyte.

That I have doon, it is thyself to wyte,

Foryeve it me, and that I thee biseke."

And yet eftsoones I hitte hym on the cheke,

815   And seyde, 'Theef, thus muchel am I wreke;

Now wol I dye, I may no lenger speke.'

But atte laste, with muchel care and wo,

We fille acorded by us selven two.

He yaf me al the bridel in myn hond,

820   To han the governance of hous and lond,

And of his tonge, and of his hond also,

And made hym brenne his book anon right tho.

And whan that I hadde geten unto me

By maistrie, al the soveraynetee,

825   And that he seyde, 'Myn owene trewe wyf,

Do as thee lust the terme of al thy lyf,

Keepe thyn honour, and keep eek myn estaat,' -

After that day we hadden never debaat.

God help me so, I was to hym as kynde

830   As any wyf from Denmark unto Ynde,

[Such] that he fell backwards into our fire.

800 And he stood up like an enraged lion,

And with his fist he struck me on the head

That I lay on the floor, as if I was dead.

And when he saw how still I lay,

He was terrified, and would have run away,

805 Until at last, I came out of my swoon:

'Oh, have you slain me, false thief?' I said,

'And have you thus murdered me for my land?

I want to kiss you before I die.'

He came near to me and knelt down,

810 And said: "Dear sister Alison,

So help me God, I will never strike you [again];

What I have done, it is you who is to blame,

Forgive me for it, I beseech you!"

And immediately after I hit him on the cheek,

815 And said: 'Thief, by this much I am avenged!

Now I will die; I can no longer speak!"

But at last, with much effort and sorrow,

We two were reconciled between ourselves.

He gave me all the bridle reins in my hand,

820 To have control over the house and land;

And also over his tongue and his hand;

And made him burn his book, right there and then!

And when I had thereby gathered unto myself

By mastery, all the sovereign [power],

825 And that he said: 'My own true wife,

Do as you please for the rest of your life,

Guard your own honour and also guard my social status' -

After that day we never argued.

God so help me, I was as kind to him

830 As any wife from Denmark to India,

And also trewe, and so was he to me.

I prey to God, that sit in magestee,

So blesse his soule for his mercy deere.

Now wol I seye my tale, if ye wol heere.

Biholde the wordes bitwene the Somonour and the Frere.

835 The Frere lough whan he hadde herd al this.-

"Now dame," quod he, "so have I joye or blis,

This is a long preamble of a tale."

And whan the Somonour herde the Frere gale,

"Lo," quod the Somonour, "Goddes armes two,

840 A frere wol entremette hym everemo.

Lo goode men, a flye and eek a frere

Wol falle in every dyssh and eek mateere.

What spekestow of preambulacioun?

What, amble, or trotte, or pees, or go sit doun,

845 Thou lettest oure disport in this manere."

"Ye, woltow so, sire Somonour?" quod the Frere,

"Now by my feith, I shal er that I go

Telle of a somonour swich a tale or two

That alle the folk shal laughen in this place."

850 "Now elles, frere, I bishrewe thy face,"

Quod this Somonour, "and I bishrewe me,

But if I telle tales two or thre

Of freres, er I come to Sidyngborne,

That I shal make thyn herte for to morne,

855 For wel I woot thy pacience in gon."

Oure Hooste cride, "Pees, and that anon!"

And seyde, "lat the womman telle hire tale,

Ye fare as folk that dronken were of ale.

Do, dame, telle forth youre tale, and that is best."

And also faithful, as he was to me.

I pray to God, who sits in majesty,

To bless his soul by His dear mercy.

Now will I tell my tale, if you will listen.

Consider the words between the Summoner and the Friar

835   The Friar laughed when he had heard all this.-

"Now lady," he said, "so have I joy or bliss,

This is a long introduction to a tale!"

And when the Summoner heard the friar's interruption,

"Lo," said the Summoner, "by God's two arms!

840   A friar will always interfere,

Behold, good men, a housefly and also a friar

Will fall into every dish and also into every subject.

What can you say say about preambling?

What! Amble or trot, hold your peace, or go sit down;

845   In this way, you are stopping our fun."

"Yes, is that what you say, sir Summoner?" said the Friar,

"Now by my faith I shall, before I go,

Tell a tale or two about a Summoner such

That all the folk in this place shall laugh.'

850   "Otherwise, Friar, I will curse your face,"

The Summoner said, "and curse me,

Unless I tell two or three tales

Of friars, before I reach Sittingbourne,

That will make your heart grieve,

855   For I know very well that your patience is gone."

Our host cried out, "Peace, and that means now!"

And said: "Let the woman tell her tale,

You act like people who are drunk with ale.

Do, lady, tell your tale, and that is best."

860	"Al redy, sire," quod she, "right as yow lest,
	If I have licence of this worthy Frere."
	"Yis, dame," quod he, "tel forth, and I wol heere."

Heere endeth the Wyf of Bathe hir Prologe.

Heere bigynneth the Tale of the Wyf of Bathe.

	In th'olde dayes of the Kyng Arthour,
	Of which that Britons speken greet honour,
865	All was this land fulfild of fayerye.
	The elf-queene, with hir joly compaignye,
	Daunced ful ofte in many a grene mede.
	This was the olde opinion, as I rede;
	I speke of manye hundred yeres ago.
870	But now kan no man se none elves mo,
	For now the grete charitee and prayeres
	Of lymytours and othere hooly freres,
	That serchen every lond and every streem,
	As thikke as motes in the sonne-beem,
875	Blessynge halles, chambres, kichenes, boures,
	Citees, burghes, castels, hye toures,
	Thropes, bernes, shipnes, dayeryes,
	This maketh that ther been no fayeryes.
	For ther as wont to walken was an elf,
880	Ther walketh now the lymytour hymself
	In undermeles and in morwenynges,
	And seyth his matyns and his hooly thynges
	As he gooth in his lymytacioun.
	Wommen may go saufly up and doun.
885	In every bussh or under every tree
	Ther is noon oother incubus but he,

860   *"All ready, sir," said she, "as you desire,*

If I have this worthy Friar's permission."

"Yes, lady," he said, "continue and I will listen."

Here ends the Wife of Bath's Prologue

Here Begins the Wife of Bath's Tale

Now in the old days of King Arthur,

Of whom Britons speak with great honour,

865   *All this land was filled with elves and fairies.*

The elf-queen, with her jolly company,

Often danced on many a green meadow.

As I interpret, this was the opinion in olden times;

I speak of many hundred years ago.

870   *But now it is known that no man can see elves anymore.*

For now, the great charity and prayers

Of licensed friar-beggars and other holy friars,

Who search every land and every stream,

As thick as dust in a beam of sunlight,

875   *Blessing halls, rooms, kitchens, bedrooms,*

Cities, towns, castles, high towers,

Manors, barns, stables and dairies,

This causes that there are now no fairies.

For where an elf was accustomed to walk,

880   *The licensed friar-beggar now walks [instead]*

At midday and in the mornings,

Saying his matins and his prayers

As he goes around his licensed district.

Women may [now] go safely all the time,

885   *In every bush or under every tree*

There is no other evil spirit, but he,

And he ne wol doon hem but dishonour.

And so bifel it that this kyng Arthour

Hadde in his hous a lusty bacheler,

890   That on a day cam ridynge fro ryver;

And happed that, allone as she was born,

He saugh a mayde walkynge hym biforn,

Of whiche mayde anon, maugree hir heed,

By verray force he rafte hir maydenhed;

895   For which oppressioun was swich clamour

And swich pursute unto the kyng Arthour,

That dampned was this knyght for to be deed,

By cours of lawe, and sholde han lost his heed -

Paraventure, swich was the statut tho -

900   But that the queene and othere ladyes mo

So longe preyeden the kyng of grace,

Til he his lyf hym graunted in the place,

And yaf hym to the queene al at hir wille,

To chese wheither she wolde hym save or spille.

905   The queene thanketh the kyng with al hir myght,

And after this thus spak she to the knyght,

Whan that she saugh hir tyme, upon a day,

"Thou standest yet," quod she, "in swich array

That of thy lyf yet hastow no suretee.

910   I grante thee lyf, if thou kanst tellen me

What thyng is it that wommen moost desiren.

Be war and keep thy nekke-boon from iren!

And if thou kanst nat tellen it anon,

Yet shal I yeve thee leve for to gon

915   A twelf-month and a day to seche and leere

An answere suffisant in this mateere;

And suretee wol I han, er that thou pace,

Thy body for to yelden in this place."

And he would not do them any harm except dishonour.

And so it happened that this King Arthur

Had a lusty bachelor in his house,

890 Who, one day, came riding from the falconry;

And happened that, as alone as [when] she was born,

He saw a maiden walking ahead of him,

From whom, immediately and despite of her resistance,

He took her virginity by sheer force;

895 For which violation was there such an outcry

And such an appeal to King Arthur,

That this knight was condemned to death,

[Who], by course of law, should have lost his head-

As, perhaps, such was then the law -

900 But the queen and the other ladies as well

Begged the king to show mercy,

Until he eventually agreed to spare his life right there,

And gave him to the queen, at her own will,

To choose whether she would save him or put to death.

905 The queen thanked the king with all her heart,

And after this, she then spoke to the knight,

One day, when she saw her chance,

"You stand yet," she said, "in such a poor state

That your life has no certainty.

910 I will grant you life if you can tell me

What thing it is that women most desire.

Be wise and save your neck from the iron [axe]!

And if you cannot tell it me straightaway,

Then I shall give you permission to be gone [for]

915 A year and a day, to seek out and learn

A satisfactory answer in this matter;

[But} I will have a guarantee before you leave,

That you will return here [at that time]."

Wo was this knyght, and sorwefully he siketh;
920 But what! He may nat do al as hym liketh.
And at the laste he chees hym for to wende,
And come agayn right at the yeres ende,
With swich answere as God wolde hym purveye;
And taketh his leve, and wendeth forth his weye.
925 He seketh every hous and every place
Where as he hopeth for to fynde grace
To lerne what thyng wommen loven moost;
But he ne koude arryven in no coost
Wher as he myghte fynde in this mateere
930 Two creatures accordynge in-feere.
Somme seyde, wommen loven best richesse,
Somme seyde honour, somme seyde jolynesse,
Somme riche array, somme seyden lust abedde,
And oftetyme to be wydwe and wedde.
935 Somme seyde, that oure hertes been moost esed
Whan that we been yflatered and yplesed.
He gooth ful ny the sothe, I wol nat lye,
A man shal wynne us best with flaterye;
And with attendance and with bisynesse
940 Been we ylymed, bothe moore and lesse.
And somme seyen, how that we loven best
For to be free, and do right as us lest,
And that no man repreve us of oure vice,
But seye that we be wise, and nothyng nyce.
945 For trewely, ther is noon of us alle,
If any wight wol clawe us on the galle,
That we nel kike; for he seith us sooth;
Assay, and he shal fynde it that so dooth.
For, be we never so vicious withinne,
950 We sol been holden wise, and clene of synne.

This knight was grieved, and sighed sorrowfully;

920 But he [knew] that he could not do as he pleased.

And at last, he chose to depart,

And to return exactly at the year's end,

With such an answer as God might provide for him;

And taking his leave, he went forth on his way.

925 He sought out every house and every place

Wherein he hoped to find the good fortune

To learn what women love the most;

But he could not arrive in any region

Where he found, in relation to this matter

930 Two persons who agreed with each other.

Some said that women loved wealth the best,

Some said, high reputation, some said gaiety,

Some, fine clothes, some said lust in bed,

And to be often widowed and re-married.

935 Some said, that our hearts are most refreshed

When we are flattered and pleased.

I will not lie, he got very close to the truth,

A man may win us best with flattery;

And with attention and with care

940 Is how we are all caught, whether rich or poor.

And some say, too, what we love the best [is]

To be free to do as we please,

And that no man reproaches us for our faults,

But to say that we are wise, and not foolish.

945 For truly there is not one of us,

If anyone shall rub us on a sore spot,

That will not kick back, since he tells the truth.

Try, and he shall find this will happen.

For, no matter how wicked we are on the inside,

950 We want to be thought of as being wise and without sin.

And somme seyn, that greet delit han we

For to been holden stable and eek secree,

And in o purpos stedefastly to dwelle,

And nat biwreye thyng that men us telle.

955 But that tale is nat worth a rake-stele,

Pardee, we wommen konne no thyng hele.

Witnesse on Myda, - wol ye heere the tale?

Ovyde, amonges othere thynges smale,

Seyde Myda hadde under his longe heres

960 Growynge upon his heed two asses eres,

The whiche vice he hydde, as he best myghte,

Ful subtilly from every mannes sighte,

That, save his wyf, ther wiste of it namo.

He loved hire moost and trusted hir also;

965 He preyede hire, that to no creature

She sholde tellen of his disfigure.

She swoor him nay, for al this world to wynne,

She nolde do that vileynye or synne,

To make hir housbonde han so foul a name.

970 She nolde nat telle it for hir owene shame.

But nathelees, hir thoughte that she dyde,

That she so longe sholde a conseil hyde;

Hir thoughte it swal so soore aboute hir herte

That nedely som word hir moste asterte;

975 And sith she dorste telle it to no man,

Doun to a mareys faste by she ran,

Til she cam there, hir herte was a fyre,

And as a bitore bombleth in the myre,

She leyde hir mouth unto the water doun:

980 "Biwreye me nat, thou water, with thy soun,"

Quod she, "to thee I telle it and namo,

Myn housbonde hath longe asses erys two!

And some say that we take great delight

To be regarded as reliable and also as discrete,

And in one purpose to continue steadfastly,

And not betray anything that men may tell us.

955 *But that tale is not worth a rake's handle,*

By God, we women cannot hide anything.

Witness King Midas. Do you want to hear the tale?

Ovid, among other small matters,

Said Midas had beneath his long hair

960 *Two ass's ears growing on his head,*

A defect which he hid, as best as he could,

Very skilfully from everyone's sight,

That, except his wife, there was no-one else who knew about it.

He loved her greatly, and also trusted her;

965 *And entreated her that, to no creature*

Would she tell about his disfigurement.

She swore to him that, not even to gain the whole world,

Would she commit that dishonour or sin,

To make her husband have such a bad reputation.

970 *Nor would she tell it due to her own deep shame.*

Nevertheless, she thought she would die,

Having to keep a secret for so long;

She thought that it swelled so sorely around her heart

That some word must surely slip from her mouth;

975 *And since she dared to tell no man,*

She ran down to a nearby marsh,

Her heart was on fire until she arrived there,

And like a bittern booming in the muddy banks,

She lowered her mouth down to the water:

980 *"Betray me not, you water, with your sound,"*

She said, "I tell it to none else but you,

My husband has two long asses' ears!

Now is myn herte al hool, now is it oute.

I myghte no lenger kepe it, out of doute."

985 Heere may ye se, thogh we a tyme abyde,

Yet out it moot, we kan no conseil hyde.

The remenant of the tale, if ye wol heere,

Redeth Ovyde, and ther ye may it leere.

This knyght, of which my tale is specially,

990 Whan that he saugh he myghte nat come therby,

This is to seye, what wommen love moost,

Withinne his brest ful sorweful was the goost.

But hoom he gooth, he myghte nat sojourne;

The day was come that homward moste he tourne.

995 And in his wey it happed hym to ryde,

In al this care under a forest syde,

Wher as he saugh upon a daunce go

Of ladyes foure and twenty, and yet mo;

Toward the whiche daunce he drow ful yerne,

1000 In hope that som wysdom sholde he lerne.

But certeinly, er he came fully there,

Vanysshed was this daunce, he nyste where.

No creature saugh he that bar lyf,

Save on the grene he saugh sittynge a wyf -

1005 A fouler wight ther may no man devyse.

Agayn the knyght this olde wyf gan ryse,

And seyde, "Sire knyght, heer forth ne lith no wey.

Tel me what that ye seken, by your fey!

Paraventure it may the bettre be,

1010 Thise olde folk kan muchel thyng," quod she.

"My leeve mooder," quod this knyght, "certeyn

I nam but deed, but if that I kan seyn

What thyng it is, that wommen moost desire.

Koude ye me wisse, I wolde wel quite youre hire."

Now that is out, my heart is now at ease.

Without doubt, I could no longer keep it [secret]."

985   *Here may you see, though we may wait for a while,*

Yet it must come out, we do not know how to hide any secret.

If you want to hear the rest of this tale,

Read Ovid, and you may learn about it there.

This knight, who is the subject of my tale,

990   *When he saw that he might not come by it,*

That is to say, the thing that women love most,

He had a very sorrowful spirit within his breast.

But could not delay any longer from going home;

[Since] the day had come when he must turn homeward.

995   *And on his way he happened to ride,*

With all care under a forest's edge,

Where he saw a dance going on

Of twenty-four ladies, maybe more;

Towards which dance he turned eagerly,

1000   *In hope that he should learn some wisdom.*

But truly, before he fully arrived there,

The dancers all vanished, he knew not where.

He saw no creature that showed sign of life,

Except an old wife sitting in a field -

1005   *No man could imagine an uglier person.*

Before the knight arrived, this old wife arose,

And said: "Sir knight, from here on there is no path.

By your faith!, Tell me what thing you are seeking.

Perhaps it would be for the better;

1010   *[Since] these old folk know many things," she said.*

"My dear mother," said this knight, "It is certain that

"I am as good as dead, unless I know to say

What thing it is that women desire most.

Could you guide me, I will repay you well."

1015   "Plight me thy trouthe, heere in myn hand," quod she,
       "The nexte thyng that I requere thee,
          Thou shalt it do, if it lye in thy myght,
          And I wol telle it yow, er it be nyght."
          "Have heer my trouthe," quod the knyght, "I grante."
1020   "Thanne," quod she, "I dar me wel avante
          Thy lyf is sauf; for I wol stonde therby,
          Upon my lyf, the queene wol seye as I.
          Lat se which is the proudeste of hem alle,
          That wereth on a coverchief or a calle,
1025   That dar seye nay of that I shal thee teche.
          Lat us go forth withouten lenger speche."
          Tho rowned she a pistel in his ere,
          And bad hym to be glad and have no fere.
          Whan they be comen to the court, this knyght
1030   Seyde he had holde his day, as he hadde hight,
          And redy was his answere, as he sayde.
          Ful many a noble wyf, and many a mayde,
          And many a wydwe, for that they been wise,
          The queene hirself sittynge as a justise,
1035   Assembled been, his answere for to heere;
          And afterward this knyght was bode appeere.
          To every wight comanded was silence,
          And that the knyght sholde telle in audience
          What thyng that worldly wommen loven best.
1040   This knyght ne stood nat stille as doth a best,
          But ot his questioun anon answerde
          With manly voys, that al the court it herde:
          "My lige lady, generally," quod he,
          "Wommen desiren to have sovereynetee
1045   As wel over hir housbond as hir love,
          And for to been in maistrie hym above.

1015	*"Pledge your word, here in my hand" she said,*
	"The next thing that I require from you,
	"You shall do it, if it lies within your power,
	And I will answer you, before it is night."
	"Have my pledge here," said the knight. "I grant it [to you]."
1020	*"Then," she said, "of this I make my boast*
	Your life is safe; for I will stand thereby,
	Upon my life, the queen will say as I.
	Let us see which is the proudest of them all,
	That wears her kerchief or a hairnet,
1025	*That dares say 'no' to what I shall teach you.*
	Let us now go without further words."
	Then, she whispered a message in his ear,
	And told him to be happy and have no fear.
	When they arrived at the court, this knight
1030	*Said he had kept his appointment, as he had promised,*
	And said he was ready with his answer.
	Many noble wives and many maidens,
	And many widows, because they be so wise,
	[With] the queen herself sitting as judge,
1035	*Were assembled to hear his answer;*
	And then the knight was summoned to appear.
	Every person was commanded to be silent,
	And that the knight should tell the audience
	What thing that worldly women love best.
1040	*This knight did not stand like a dumb beast,*
	But answered this question immediately
	With a manly voice, so that the entire court heard it:
	My liege lady, across the world," he said,
	"Women desire to have sovereignty
1045	*Over both their husband as well as over their love,*
	And to have mastery over him.

This is youre mooste desir, thogh ye me kille.

Dooth as yow list, I am heer at youre wille."

In al the court ne was ther wyf, ne mayde,

1050   Ne wydwe, that contraried that he sayde,

But seyden he was worthy han his lyf.

And with that word up stirte the olde wyf,

Which that the knyght saugh sittynge in the grene.

"Mercy," quod she, "my sovereyn lady queene,

1055   Er that youre court departe, do me right.

I taughte this answere unto the knyght,

For which he plighte me his trouthe there,

The firste thyng I wolde of hym requere,

He wolde it do, if it lay in his myght.

1060   Bifor the court thanne preye I thee, sir knyght,"

Quod she, "that thou me take unto thy wyf,

For wel thou woost that I have kept thy lyf.

If I seye fals, sey nay, upon thy fey!"

This knyght answerde, "Allas and weylawey!

1065   I woot right wel that swich was my biheste!

For Goddes love, as chees a newe requeste!

Taak al my good, and lat my body go!"

"Nay, thanne," quod she, "I shrewe us bothe two!

For thogh that I be foul, and oold, and poore,

1070   I nolde for al the metal, ne for oore,

That under erthe is grave, or lith above,

But if thy wyf I were, and eek thy love."

"My love?" quod he, "nay, my dampnacioun!

Allas, that any of my nacioun

1075   Sholde evere so foule disparaged be!"

But al for noght, the ende is this, that he

Constreyned was, he nedes moste hir wedde;

And taketh his olde wyf, and gooth to bedde.

This is your greatest desire, though you may kill me.

Do as you wish, I am here subject to your will."

In all the court there was not one wife, or maiden,

1050 *Or widow who contradicted what he had said,*

But all said, he was worthy to have his life.

And with that word up stood the old wife,

Whom he had seen sitting in the field.

"Mercy," she cried, "my sovereign lady queen!

1055 *Before your court departs, give me justice.*

I who taught this answer to the knight,

For which he pledged his word to me, out there,

The first thing I would require of him,

He would do it, if it lay in his power.

1060 *Before the court, then, ask I you, sir knight,"*

She said, "that you will take me as your wife,

For you know very well that I have saved your life.

If I speak falsely, say 'no', upon your faith!"

This knight replied: "Alas and woe!

1065 *I know full well that I made such a promise!*

[But] for God's love, choose a new request!

Take all my wealth and let my body go [free]."

"No, then," said she, "I curse us both!

For though I may be disgusting and old and poor,

1070 *I will not, for all the metal, nor for the ore,*

That is buried under the earth, or lies above it,

[Be] anything except your wife and your true love."

"My love?" he said, "No, my damnation!

Alas! that anyone of my station

1075 *Should ever be so foully dishonoured!"*

But all this was for nothing, the conclusion is that he

Was compelled by necessity, and must wed her;

And take his old wife and go to bed.

Now wolden som men seye, paraventure,

1080 That for my necligence I do no cure

To tellen yow the joye and al th'array,

That at the feeste was that ilke day;

To whiche thyng shortly answere I shal:

I seye, ther nas no joye ne feeste at al;

1085 Ther nas but hevynesse and muche sorwe.

For prively he wedde hir on a morwe,

And al day after hidde hym as an owle,

So wo was hym, his wyf looked so foule.

Greet was the wo the knyght hadde in his thoght,

1090 Whan he was with his wyf abedde ybroght;

He walweth and he turneth to and fro.

His olde wyf lay smylynge everemo,

And seyde, "O deere housbonde, benedicitee,

Fareth every knyght thus with his wyf, as ye?

1095 Is this the lawe of Kyng Arthures hous?

Is every knyght of his so dangerous?

I am youre owene love and youre wyf;

I am she which that saved hath youre lyf.

And certes, yet dide I yow nevere unright;

1100 Why fare ye thus with me this firste nyght?

Ye faren lyk a man had lost his wit.

What is my gilt? For Goddes love, tel it,

And it shal been amended, if I may."

"Amended," quod this knyght, "allas! nay! nay!

1105 It wol nat been amended nevere mo;

Thou art so loothly and so oold also,

And therto comen of so lough a kynde,

That litel wonder is thogh I walwe and wynde.

So wolde God, myn herte wolde breste!"

1110 "Is this," quod she, "the cause of youre unreste?"

Now, perhaps, some men might say,

1080 *That, I am negligent in not taking care*

To tell you about the joy and all the preparations,

Which were seen at the celebrations that same day;

To this thing, I shall give you a brief answer:

I say, there was no joy or feast at all;

1085 *There was only heaviness [of heart] and great sorrow.*

For he wedded her in private the next morning,

And for all day afterwards, he hid himself away like an owl,

As he was sorrowful that his wife looked so ugly.

The knight's thoughts were full of great woe,

1090 *When he was brought to bed with his wife;*

He tossed and turned backwards and forwards.

His old wife lay there, smiling continuously,

And said: "O my dear husband, God bless!

Does every knight conduct himself thus with his wife, as you?

1095 *Is this the custom in King Arthur's house?*

Are knights of his all so disdainful?

I am your own true love and your wife;

I am she who has saved your very life.

And truly, I have never done you any wrong;

1100 *[So] why behave like this with me on the first night?*

You act like a man who has lost his mind.

What is my crime? For the love of God tell it to me,

And it shall be corrected, if I can."

"Corrected," said this knight, "Alas, nay, nay!

1105 *It will not be corrected for ever more;*

You are so loathsome, and also so old,

And come from such a low ancestry,

It is little wonder that I toss and turn.

So would that God would make my heart burst!"

1110 *"Is this," she said, "the cause of your distress?"*

"Ye certeinly," quod he, "no wonder is!"

"Now, sire," quod she, "I koude amende al this,

If that me liste, er it were dayes thre,

So wel ye myghte bere yow unto me.

1115   But for ye speken of swich gentillesse

As is descended out of old richesse,

That therfore sholden ye be gentil men,

Swich arrogance nis nat worth an hen.

Looke who that is moost vertuous alway,

1120   Pryvee and apert, and moost entendeth ay

To do the gentil dedes that he kan,

Taak hym for the grettest gentil man.

Crist wole we clayme of hym oure gentillesse,

Nat of oure eldres for hire old richesse.

1125   For thogh they yeve us al hir heritage,

For which we clayme to been of heigh parage,

Yet may they nat biquethe, for no thyng

To noon of us hir vertuous lyvyng,

That made hem gentil men ycalled be,

1130   And bad us folwen hem in swich degree.

Wel kan the wise poete of Florence,

That highte Dant, speken in this sentence.

Lo in swich maner rym is Dantes tale:

`Ful selde upriseth by his branches smale

1135   Prowesse of man, for God of his goodnesse,

Wole, that of hym we clayme oure gentillesse.'

For of oure eldres may we no thyng clayme

But temporel thyng, that man may hurte and mayme.

Eek every wight woot this as wel as I,

1140   If gentillesse were planted natureelly

Unto a certeyn lynage doun the lyne,

Pryvee nor apert, thanne wolde they nevere fyne

"Yes, truly," he said, "and it is no wonder!"

"Now, sir," she said, "I could correct all this,

If I wished, before three days have passed,

Provided that you behave well to me.

1115 "But as you speak about such [high] nobility

That is descended from old wealth,

You should therefore be a noble man,

[However] such arrogance is worthless.

Look at who is always the most virtuous,

1120 In private or public, and [who] tries most hard

To do the noble deeds that he knows,

Take him to be the greatest gentleman.

Christ wills us to claim our nobility from Him,

Not from our ancestors for their old wealth.

1125 For although they give us all their heritage,

From which we claim to be of high descent,

Yet they may not bequeath any

Of their virtues to any of us,

That made them be called noble gentlemen,

1130 And ordered us follow them in every such way.

Well knows that wise poet from Florence,

Who is called Dante, speaks on this matter.

Look, Dante's tale says in this manner of rhyme

'It is seldom that, [any] further along a family tree,

1135 Will a man's excellence extend; for God, in his goodness.

Wishes us to claim our nobility from Him',

Since, from our ancestors, we can claim nothing

But worldly things, with which man may hurt and injure.

Also, every person knows this as well as I,

1140 That if nobility was implanted by nature

Into the line of a particular family,

They would never refrain, in public or private,

To doon of gentillesse the faire office,

They myghte do no vileynye or vice.

1145 Taak fyr, and ber it in the derkeste hous

Bitwix this and the mount of Kaukasous,

And lat men shette the dores and go thenne;

Yet wole the fyr as faire lye and brenne

As twenty thousand men myghte it biholde;

1150 His office natureel ay wol it holde,

Up peril of my lyf, til that it dye.

Heere may ye se wel, how that genterye

Is nat annexed to possessioun,

Sith folk ne doon hir operacioun

1155 Alwey, as dooth the fyr, lo, in his kynde.

For God it woot, men may wel often fynde

A lordes sone do shame and vileynye,

And he that wole han pris of his gentrye,

For he was boren of a gentil hous,

1160 And hadde hise eldres noble and vertuous,

And nel hym-selven do no gentil dedis,

Ne folwen his gentil auncestre that deed is,

He nys nat gentil, be he duc or erl;

For vileyns synful dedes make a cherl.

1165 For gentillesse nys but renomee

Of thyne auncestres for hire heigh bountee,

Which is a strange thyng to thy persone.

Thy gentillesse cometh fro God allone.

Thanne comth oure verray gentillesse of grace,

1170 It was no thyng biquethe us with oure place.

Thenketh hou noble, as seith Valerius,

Was thilke Tullius Hostillius,

That out of poverte roos to heigh noblesse.

Reedeth Senek, and redeth eek Boece,

From performing their duties of nobility,

[That] they would never commit dishonour or sin.

1145   *Take fire and carry it into the darkest house*

Between here and the Mount of Caucasus,

And let men shut their doors and go thenceforth [away];

Yet the fire will [continue to] blaze and burn

As if twenty thousand men were watching;

1150   *It will always perform its natural function,*

I swear upon my life, until it dies.

Here you can see that nobility

Is not related to possessions,

Since folk do not behave

1155   *According to nature, as the fire always does.*

For God knows, men may very often find

A lord's son committing shame and dishonour;

And he that praises his own nobility,

Because of being born to some noble house,

1160   *And had noble and virtuous ancestors,*

And will do none of those noble deeds himself,

Nor follow [the example] of his deceased noble ancestors,

He is not noble, [whether] he be a duke or an earl;

For villainous, sinful deeds make a man a peasant.

1165   *Nobility is nothing but renown*

Of your ancestors for their great virtue,

Which is an alien thing to your person.

Your nobility comes from God alone.

Thence comes our true nobility by [His] grace,

1170   *It was not bequeathed to us with our title or rank.*

Think how noble, as Valerius said,

Was that same Tullius Hostilius,

Who rose out of poverty to high nobility.

Read Seneca, and also read Boethius,

1175 Ther shul ye seen expres that it no drede is,

That he is gentil that dooth gentil dedis.

And therfore, leeve housbonde, I thus conclude:

Al were it that myne auncestres weren rude,

Yet may the hye God, and so hope I,

1180 Grante me grace to lyven vertuously.

Thanne am I gentil whan that I bigynne

To lyven vertuously, and weyve synne.

And ther as ye of poverte me repreeve,

The hye God, on whom that we bileeve,

1185 In wilful poverte chees to lyve his lyf.

And certes every man, mayden or wyf,

May understonde that Jesus, hevene kyng,

Ne wolde nat chesen vicious lyvyng.

Glad poverte is an honeste thyng, certeyn,

1190 This wole Senec and othere clerkes seyn.

Who so that halt hym payd of his poverte,

I holde hym riche, al hadde he nat a sherte.

He that coveiteth is a povre wight,

For he wolde han that is nat in his myght;

1195 But he that noght hath, ne coveiteth have,

Is riche, although ye holde hym but a knave.

Verray poverte, it syngeth proprely;

Juvenal seith of poverte myrily:

`The povre man, whan he goth by the weye,

1200 Bifore the theves he may synge and pleye.'

Poverte is hateful good, and, as I gesse,

A ful greet bryngere out of bisynesse;

A greet amender eek of sapience

To hym that taketh it in pacience.

1205 Poverte is this, although it seme alenge,

Possessioun, that no wight wol chalenge.

1175	There, you shall see clearly, there is no doubt,
	That he is noble who does noble deeds.
	And therefore, dear husband, I thus conclude:
	That although my ancestors were of low birth,
	So I hope that yet may the high God,
1180	Grant me the favour to live virtuously.
	Then I am noble when I begin
	To live virtuously, and eschew sin.
	And whereas you reproach me for my poverty,
	The high God, in whom we believe,
1185	Chose freely to live his life in poverty.
	And certainly, every man, or maiden, or wife,
	May understand that Jesus, Heaven's king,
	Would not have chosen a wicked way of living.
	Truly, cheerful poverty is an honest thing,
1190	Which Seneca and other scholars say.
	Whosoever is satisfied with his poverty,
	I consider him to be rich, although he has not [even] a shirt.
	He who covets is a poor person,
	For he would have that which is not in his power;
1195	But he that has nothing, nor desires to have [anything],
	Is rich, even though you consider him as only a servant.
	True poverty, sings its own song;
	Juvenal merrily speaks about poverty:
	"The poor man, when he goes along the way,
1200	Before the robbers he can sing and play."
	Poverty is a horrible good, and, as I guess,
	It is a great remover of concerns;
	And is also great improver of wisdom
	For him that takes it in with patience.
1205	Poverty is this, although it seems wretched,
	It is a possession that no other person wants.

Poverte ful ofte, whan a man is lowe,

Maketh his God and eek hymself to knowe.

Poverte a spectacle is, as thynketh me,

1210 Thurgh which he may hise verray freendes see.

And therfore, sire, syn that I noght yow greve,

Of my poverte namoore ye me repreve.

Now sire, of elde ye repreve me,

And certes, sire, thogh noon auctoritee

1215 Were in no book, ye gentils of honour

Seyn, that men sholde an oold wight doon favour,

And clepe hym fader for youre gentillesse;

And auctours shal I fynden, as I gesse.

Now, ther ye seye that I am foul and old,

1220 Than drede you noght to been a cokewold;

For filthe and eelde, al so moot I thee,

Been grete wardeyns upon chastitee;

But nathelees, syn I knowe youre delit,

I shal fulfille youre worldly appetit."

1225 "Chese now," quod she, "oon of thise thynges tweye:

To han me foul and old til that I deye,

And be to yow a trewe humble wyf,

And nevere yow displese in al my lyf;

Or elles ye wol han me yong and fair,

1230 And take youre aventure of the repair

That shal be to youre hous, by cause of me,

Or in som oother place may wel be.

Now chese yourselven wheither that yow liketh."

This knyght avyseth hym and sore siketh,

1235 But atte laste, he seyde in this manere:

"My lady and my love, and wyf so deere,

I put me in youre wise governance.

Cheseth yourself, which may be moost plesance

When a man is [so] humbled, poverty very often,

Makes him know his God and also himself.

It seems to me that poverty is an eye-glass,

1210 *Through which a man may see his true friends.*

And therefore, sir, since I have not brought you grief,

You should no longer reproach me for my poverty.

Now, sir, you reproach me for being old;

And truly, sir, although there is no authority

1215 *In any book, you gentlemen of honour*

Say that men should show respect to the aged,

And call him father, due to your nobility;

I believe I could find authors [who agree].

Now since you say that I am ugly and old,

1220 *There is no fear of having an adulterous wife;*

For, may I prosper, foulness and old age,

Are great protectors of chastity;

But, nevertheless, since I know your delight,

I shall satisfy your worldly appetite.

1225 *"Choose, now," she said, "one of these two things:*

To have me ugly and old until I die,

And to be your true and humble wife,

And never to anger you for all my life;

Or else to have me young and beautiful,

1230 *And take your chance with the visits*

There shall be to your house, because of me,

Or in some other place, as well may be.

Now choose whichever pleases you."

This knight considered, and sighed bitterly,

1235 *But at last, he spoke in this manner:*

"My lady and my love, and wife so dear,

I put myself in your wise control.

Choose yourself whichever is the most pleasing

And moost honour to yow and me also.

1240 I do no fors the wheither of the two;

For, as yow liketh, it suffiseth me."

"Thanne have I gete of yow maistrie," quod she,

"Syn I may chese and governe as me lest?"

"Ye, certes, wyf," quod he, "I holde it best."

1245 "Kys me," quod she, "we be no lenger wrothe,

For, by my trouthe, I wol be to yow bothe!

This is to seyn, ye, bothe fair and good.

I prey to God that I moote sterven wood

But I to yow be al so good and trewe

1250 As evere was wyf, syn that the world was newe.

And but I be to-morn as fair to seene

As any lady, emperice, or queene,

That is bitwixe the est and eke the west,

Dooth with my lyf and deth right as yow lest.

1255 Cast up the curtyn, looke how that it is."

And whan the knyght saugh verraily al this,

That she so fair was, and so yong therto,

For joye he hente hire in hise armes two.

His herte bathed in a bath of blisse,

1260 A thousand tyme a-rewe he gan hir kisse,

And she obeyed hym in every thyng

That myghte doon hym plesance or likyng.

And thus they lyve unto hir lyves ende

In parfit joye;-and Jesu Crist us sende

1265 Housbondes meeke, yonge, fressh abedde,

And grace t'overbyde hem that we wedde;

And eek I praye Jesu shorte hir lyves

That nat wol be governed by hir wyves;

And olde and angry nygardes of dispence,

1270 God sende hem soone verray pestilence!

Heere endeth the Wyves Tale of Bathe.

And [brings] the most honour to you, and to me also.

1240   *I do not care which of these two;*

For if you like it, that is enough for me."

"Then I have gained mastery over you," she said,

Since may I choose and govern as I wish?"

"Yes, truly, wife," he said, "I consider that is best."

1245   *"Kiss me," she said, "we shall no longer be angry,*

For by my truth, I will be both to you!

That is to say, I will be both beautiful and good.

I pray to God that I will die insane

Unless I am not as good and true to you

1250   *As ever a was wife since the world began.*

And unless, by tomorrow morning, I am as beautiful to see

As any lady, empress, or queen,

That is, between the [furthest] east and also the [furthest] west,

Do with my life and death as you please.

1255   *Lift the curtain and see how it is."*

And when the knight truly saw all this,

That she was so very beautiful, and moreover so young,

With joy he embraced her in his two arms.

His heart bathed in a blissful bath,

1260   *He kissed her a thousand times in a row,*

And she obeyed him in everything

That might give him pleasure or sexual enjoyment.

And thus they lived to the end of their lives

In perfect joy; and Jesus Christ to send us

1265   *Husbands that are meek, young and full of vigour in bed,*

And have the good luck to outlive those whom we wed;

And I also pray Jesus to cut short the lives

Of those who will not be governed by their wives;

And to old and angry misers with their money,

1270   *May God soon send them the true plague!*

Here ends the Wife of Bath's Tale.

Made in United States
North Haven, CT
31 May 2025

69380624R00109